Silence Interrupted

Silence Interrupted

Sania Shaikh

LANIER PRESS
Alpharetta, GA

This is a work of fiction. Names, characters, businesses, places, and events are either the products of the author's imagination or are used in a fictitious manner. Any resemblance to actual persons, living or dead, or actual events is purely coincidental.

Copyright © 2016 by Sania Shaikh

All rights reserved. No part of this book may be reproduced or transmitted in any form or by any means, electronic or mechanical, including photocopying, recording, or any information storage and retrieval system, without permission in writing from the publisher. For more information, address Lanier Press, c/o BookLogix Permissions Department, 1264 Old Alpharetta Rd., Alpharetta, GA 30005.

ISBN: 978-1-61005-812-4

Library of Congress Control Number: 2016953516

10 9 8 7 6 5 4 3 2   1 1 0 3 1 6

Printed in the United States of America

∞This paper meets the requirements of ANSI/NISO Z39.48-1992 (Permanence of Paper)

To Sara Bhaldar.

Acknowledgments

I WOULD LIKE TO THANK JUDAH, URVI, AND MANISH UNCLE for reading *Silence Interrupted* and encouraging me to get it published. Thank you Akif, Mom, and Dad. Thank you Emma, Arsheen, Noora, and Griffin. Thank you to my friends and family. You have been nothing but encouraging. Lastly, I would like to thank everyone at BookLogix who helped me to get *Silence Interrupted* published.

Troye

THE HORRID THING ABOUT SLEEP IS THAT I NEVER REALIZE how much I need it until I wake up. It gets a bit more irritating—no, a lot more irritating—when I don't actually need to wake up. It's a tedious matter, and I'd rather it not have happened as it has these past few days.

I open my eyes and register a sharp rapping to my left, coming from my bedroom door. I get out of my warm cocoon of a bed and swing it open. The words are out of my mouth before I can stop them.

"Is he drunk?" I ask. There she is, with a runny nose and bloodshot eyes, puffy from crying, diminishing her usually ethereal features.

"Yes, he . . ." She can't finish her sentence because she breaks into a fresh wave of sobs. It's an uncomfortable situation—her bawling could grab my father's attention, and I can't risk that happening.

I grab her hand. "Here. Get inside," I say. I pull her into my room. I have a few water bottles and a box of tissues in case she needs to have her nightly visits. It is a necessity because she has been visiting my room more often than I'd like as of late.

Her usually smooth skin looks red and stretched, like there isn't enough skin to cover her entire form. Her deep brown eyes have lost their usual glint of mischief. Her nightdress is in tatters, the frayed hem finally giving way to worn strands.

Usually, we can evade him quickly, but he catches a glimpse of me as I'm shutting the door.

"Troye!" He sounds both angry and jovial, which is an odd combination when combined with alcohol. He's at the door before I can fully comprehend it, and I reluctantly let him in.

He staggers a couple of steps before I hear a glass shatter. I turn a lamp on, washing the room in a yellowish hue.

"What the hell?" I say. He looks embarrassed, or at least as embarrassed as you can look when you're drunk.

"Um . . ." he slurs. He knows that I have strong feelings against alcohol, and yet he still drinks himself to sleep at least three times a week. I feel vitriolic and determined to make him feel guilty, whether or not it is right considering my mother's delicate state.

"So, what did she do that was *so* important that you wake me up at *the godforsaken hour of two thirty in the morning*? And on top of that," I look at him with distaste, "you're drunk. Again. Where the hell did you get that? We threw all of yours out last week."

Squinting in the light, he stumbles through his answers. "I've got some friends at the bar, good people. They were sympathetic because I have to put up with her." He glares at my mom, and she lets out a terrified squeak. He chuckles harshly, scratching the back of his neck.

I'm silent. I didn't know he still had friends after the last time he got kicked out.

"I–I don't know what to say; I'm that pissed with you," I say honestly.

"Of course you don't, boy, and I don't like your tone . . ." He curses loudly and I'm taken aback.

Though cursing may be typical for a stereotypical alcoholic, my father didn't curse often, and it was always startling to hear it. Years ago, I would've never thought I'd ever hear him curse, but I guess times change.

Is it me, or is it that everything always deteriorates after a while? Friendships deteriorate, family bonds deteriorate. Everything that you know, everything that you love, at some point it's gone, and it will never come back—ever. That's the most horrible part about it.

"Please leave," I say firmly. "Come back when you're sober."

He doesn't say a word when he bends over to pick up the broken glass and throw it in the garbage. I'm surprised that he's so careful; he doesn't cut his hands once. Looking around, he grabs a handful of tissues from my desk and soaks up the whiskey from the floor.

He looks at me with his watery green eyes. "I wish you were never born," he says before the door can shut behind him.

"Me too," I manage to say before my voice cracks.

The next day I wake up, sunlight streaming through my still open window. I check my alarm clock—9:30 a.m., it reads. I suddenly remember the events of last night.

Feeling sort of irritated, I push the covers forward with my feet and get up. My parents are already at work, so I have the house to myself. Even though it is sweltering outside with the heat of summer setting in, I will never decline a mug of hot cocoa, and I know exactly where to go for it.

I take a quick shower, brush my teeth, and change into jeans and the blue T-shirt from my school's orchestra's trip to the Georgia Aquarium and the World of Coke in Atlanta.

I whistle as I practically fly down the stairs. I keep a secret stash of those disgusting hot cocoa packets behind my mother's spice rack. They taste wretched, more like cardboard than chocolate, but I never seem to mind that. It makes me feel a bit young, as if I'm not going to be going into my senior year in a few months.

And besides, anything tastes better than coffee to me. It tastes of taxes and mortgage and all the other hassles that adults have in their lives. I don't really want to deal with that.

After setting the now-washed mug on the drying rack, I run up the stairs three at a time.

I don't believe in walking up stairs normally because I feel it's a waste of time. Just like life is too short for doing something you don't like doing, life is too short for climbing up the stairs normally.

I fall onto my bed and sigh. This heat paired with the alcoholic tendencies of my father indicates that this summer will be excruciatingly long.

3

Adelaide

I TRULY UNDERSTOOD HOW SCREWED I WAS WHEN MY SCHOOL sent a letter to my parents. It had a lot of pretentious words, but it basically meant that my GPA would be dropped significantly because of my Calculus grade. I had, unlike most, taken Calculus during eleventh grade, sitting in with a class of seniors.

Of course, I knew how horrible my grade was before the letter came. I had it all planned out—how I would fix it. That's what I always do. I screw things up, and then I fix them.

If I were a Time Lord on BBC's *Doctor Who*, I'd be The Fixer. There are three things wrong with this conclusion, though. One, I am not from the Planet Gallifrey; two, I am not European, or at least the European equivalent of Gallifrey, and I don't have one of those accents; and three, being a Fixer isn't an occupation.

But who cares? "Hello! I'm the Fixer."

On second thought, that sounds pathetic. If I was actually an alien with age-defying looks, I wouldn't be in this situation.

This year, I should focus on an extracurricular that boosts my college résumé. I play the violin. Yes, I know, some people say that the violin is the "most generic instrument" of the orchestra. I really don't care. The violin is pretty awesome, especially mine. It's black, and the sound quality is immeasurable.

I know some people who could be musical geniuses, but the word prodigy definitely doesn't fit me. I can play okay but not wonderfully. I can't play the way that can make someone cry in a matter of minutes, nor with the kind of movements that can make someone feel something indescribable.

I've heard people talk about their favorite musicians and conductors. "Not a dry eye in the house," they'd say, lost in memories. I never believed that when I was young. I would imagine an auditorium the size of a football field. It would have plushy red-violet seats in case someone who was disinterested wanted to go to sleep. The orchestra would start to play, and the first ones to cry would be the ladies with the expensive hairdos in the front row, even though they wouldn't stop gossiping the entire time. Then, gradually, the buff man in the back row with the hidden tattoos would cry because the music reminded him of his childhood. The auditorium would start to flood because of everyone's tears. Then, the orchestra would run away because they didn't want their instruments to get wet. Awakened from their dreamlike stupor, the audience would rush out of the room, their dresses and tuxedos wet, except that one guy who was still sleeping. He'd stay asleep.

Let's just say it'd get pretty morbid. Yes, that's how my thought process functions.

My name is quite unique. I have two last names and no middle name. Basically my mom is a very . . . free-spirited person. I don't know how else to explain it. When she got married, she kept her maiden name, Lillvik, and just added it to my dad's last name. That's how I ended up with two surnames.

Personally, I'd rather be Adelaide Lillvik. Trumbull sounds so much like Trunchbull, and frankly, I don't want any connection with that hag of a teacher from *Matilda*. Roald Dahl was brilliant, but why did he have to name her Trunchbull? Why couldn't he just name her Smith? Williams? Tyler? Normal names. It'd be a lot easier for the Smiths to cope with their last name because there are so many of them. It's harder for Trunchbulls—or in my case, Trumbulls—to cope. Why? Because other than my family, Trumbulls are virtually nonexistent.

My first name, Adelaide, is a bit less complicated. My mom's best friend is named Adelaide, plus my mom likes how it sounds. She always says that it just slipped through her lips; it was like the flow of a river. I guess I'm fine with Adelaide, but you wouldn't believe how many people pronounce it wrong. It's kind of stupid. Adelaide is so easy to say, and it's growing more common.

My train of thought is interrupted by the doorbell ringing. I pull out my headphones, already missing the sound of "Tetrishead" by Zoë Keating. Before I even open the door, I can tell it's my mom by looking out of the adjacent window. I swing it open hastily, and she looks at me with an expression of deep seriousness.

"Hey Del, you know there's a new family two doors down," she says. I look at her inquisitively.

"So?" I ask. She looks around as if the new neighbors will spring out of nowhere, holding baseball bats, ready to bludgeon us to death.

"They have a son; I want you to welcome him here."

"Mom, why are you so interested in them?"

Her face falls. She leans very close to me and whispers, "They used to live down in Florida. They moved here because the father . . . he drinks. Finally got put in jail a few weeks ago. They came here for a fresh start."

Holding the burden of that new information, I walk back upstairs, wondering how this mystery boy feels. He must be broken. Many people break things. They are objects, though.

Small things like glasses, or a mug. Insignificant things. The things that most people think can be broken and the things that I think can be broken differ greatly. Humans can be broken. Me? I end up breaking myself.

If you asked most adults and parents, they'd say teenagers have absolutely nothing to worry about. Completely true, right? Incorrect. We're raging hormonal beings that try to hide both pimples and insecurity, so when we do screw up—because everyone does—we have a different way of reacting. We can't handle the sinking in our hearts. It's a pain coming from the core of our very existence, otherwise known as disappointment. We try to ease that pain, and when that doesn't work, we try to mask it. We push ourselves into trying to fix whatever went wrong.

Ah, there it is again, that accursed fixing of things. Our entire world is shaped around fixing things. People have jobs centered on fixing things: doctors fix people, car mechanics fix, well, cars. People all over the world, in their little communities, fixing things. Everyone fixes things, except those ladies that sit in the front row of the auditorium inside my head. They do absolutely nothing productive: just destruct people's self-esteem and spend their husbands' millions.

But does anyone ever think about being free? Who cares about this eternal fixing of things? People think about freedom, but do they act on it? Of course not. This world, unfortunately, is too busy to think about anything unnecessary.

I warned you that I rambled.

But really, some people look at the bigger picture. There's a book I read as a child called *When You Reach Me*. Rebecca Stead says that almost everyone is born with a veil over their eyes. This veil glazes over pretty much everything that actually matters in life. But sometimes, the veil lifts, and you see the vivid, cruelly beautiful, mesmerizing place that the world really is—but never for long.

That happens to me sometimes. Like now, as I'm sitting on my bed before the first day of senior year. For some people, these epiphanies are the highlights of their days. It's a pathetic life, in my opinion, and I can say that because it's my life that I'm talking about.

My mother is right about the presence of a new family. I haven't seen the boy, but I've seen his parents, and even so, only once, on a rare occasion when I was walking outside. Their arms were laden with groceries, and slivers of several foods could be seen at the tops of the large bags.

They looked like nice people. His mother was the epitome of what a mother should look like. Her face was full of soft curves, creating an inviting look complemented by her warm brown eyes.

His dad had cold green eyes and brown hair. His face was the opposite of his wife's—rigid and angular, full of straight lines. He looked intimidating, but then he laughed at something the woman said. All the edges disappeared, and he looked as kind and inviting as his wife.

I'll probably meet their son at school. I wonder what I should say. I can't just go up to someone and say, *Hey! My name is Adelaide. Oh, and by the way, I'm sorry that your father's developing a drinking problem! Maybe we can hang out sometime and I can pathetically attempt to console you!*

Troye

MY PARENTS ARE WAITING FOR ME.

"Troye, come sit down."

I oblige. They look at each other, attempting to gain confidence. My dad speaks first.

"Troye, we know you've . . . gone through a lot recently, and we decided that it would be . . . beneficial to you if we . . . if we moved for a while."

"What?" I ask. "What do you mean?"

My mother answers this time. "Your father has found an alternative job in Georgia. It's better this way, especially after what happened with the police last weekend."

I don't feel shocked. Over the past few weeks, my mother has caught me lying in my room, staring out of the window for hours on end. She brought home groceries once and a few hours later the pint of chocolate ice cream was missing. Three guesses who took it. I am in no mood to care that I am acting like a hormonal teenage girl.

I stand up and look at my feet, putting my hands in my pockets. "When are we leaving?"

"Two and a half weeks," my parents say simultaneously and monotonously.

"August sixth," my mom adds. "School there starts on August eleventh."

"Well, I guess I should start packing then," I say casually.

My parents look relieved that I'm not being emotional. I leave the table.

When I went to Georgia for last year's orchestra trip, it didn't look that bad to me. In fact, I really liked being in Atlanta. I hope we live close to there. Who knows, maybe this is all I need: some time to "recover."

The only word I would say to describe this neighborhood is plain. The grass is perfectly green. The sky is artificially blue. The houses are gray. Typical neighborhood, typical people.

I have conquered the second-largest bedroom in the house. It has the view of our driveway and everything in front of it, along with another window on the side of the house, facing the most majestic brick wall of the house next to us. School starts tomorrow, and I haven't been outside at all. I look out my window with the blinds drawn in a way that the view is one-sided.

I haven't seen any teenagers my age except one: a girl. She looked about sixteen or seventeen, and was quite possibly the most average-looking girl I've ever seen—fitting for this neighborhood. She had black hair and ivory skin, which was slightly red, as if she didn't go outside often. My parents were in the driveway, and I studied her studying them. Then, she walked all the way to the corner and out of sight.

I turn to my desk, my back to the windows. I haven't furnished my room yet; it is completely bare, with white walls. I hate white. It's too perfect: a flawless color with no blemishes. I have to paint this room before I start getting comfortable here. My old room back in Florida was brown.

I know what people usually think about the color brown, and they're wrong. It was a beautiful brown, a little bit darker than cinnamon. It gave my room a warm feel, even on the coldest of winter nights. But it holds painful memories now. I've decided not to repaint my walls that particular color.

It's better not to be reminded of tragedy, even if avoiding it drags you by the hair into a dark pit of general loneliness and despair. Oh, what an optimist I am. At this rate, school's going to be interesting tomorrow.

My first assessment of Rookwood High School: it is a gold mine of stereotypes. It doesn't matter where this high school is. It has the same types of people: dedicated athletes, gossiping girls who clog hallways, studious pupils who walk around immersed in textbooks yet simultaneously managing to avoid the infinite obstacles the hallways offer, etc. The student population has tight-knit groups that people rarely exit or enter, which unfortunately for me, means that it's hard to enter one.

I don't know how many times I'm going to say this, but it is typical. Nothing eventful happened in Literature, the only class I've had so far. My next class is Calculus. Calculus is the only class that I had to do a significant homework for. For summer homework, we had to complete a cumulative review packet of everything in Precalculus and a few other concepts I learned years ago. It was easy work; some of it didn't need any work at all. However, the questions clearly stated to show work.

I hate when teachers enforce a certain way to do things. Like when I took Analytic Geometry sophomore year, I could answer the questions in my head. I would just write the answers down, and the teacher took points off because I didn't show my work. If it's convenient for me to work efficiently without doing complicated steps, why can't I? I present to you: the American public school system.

I walk into the classroom, and I know I'm going to hate it here already. There are white walls, nothing to cover them except posters like "Respect Your Seniors!" and "Always Show Your Work!" The only thing that I don't hate in here is the fact that my neighbor is here.

She makes direct eye contact with me for a split second because of the noise of my footsteps. I see that her eyes are a brownish color, but the color isn't noticeable compared to her other facial attributes. Her irises are contrasted by the mild circles under her eyes. She has a narrow nose, and semi-sharp characteristics. However, the most prominent aspect of her face is the intelligence that shines through her features, as if she is much wiser and more mature than one would expect for her quantifiable age.

I head toward the seat behind her. I swear when I walk by her, I hear her mutter something unintelligible. I turn my head to look at her, but she hasn't looked up, still doing something in a white notebook. I can guess what it is, though, because I see notes of music in treble clef.

The class starts like the last class did.

"We have a new student coming all the way from Florida . . ." Mrs. Schroeder begins. She is the only one who has defied any stereotypical notions today: her voice is cold and slightly nasal, nothing like what one would think she sounds like.

After she introduces me and takes the attendance, she goes around checking the summer homework. She travels from the back row to the first. She checks my work with a disapproving nod. It's quite the oxymoron.

"Good job, Troye, dear, but next time do the work first before figuring out the answer." She hands me a new worksheet to complete by the end of class. I roll my eyes when she looks away.

Then she moves on to the girl, Adelaide, whose name I know now thanks to the trusty attendance sheet. Mrs. Schroeder looks at Adelaide's packet for a couple of seconds before tutting and putting it down.

"Adelaide, dear, why didn't you show any work on some of these problems?"

Adelaide shrugs, interlacing her fingers. "I didn't need to. I could figure it out in my head. Isn't that the goal of the school system? Efficiency?"

The teacher smiles tight-lipped, an artificial smile. "Sweetie, I'm going to have to give you a zero."

I expect Adelaide to argue, complain, or yell at Mrs. Schroeder. But what she does instead is completely unexpected. She stands up coolly, and starts reciting a poem.

> It matters not how strait the gate,
>   How charged with punishments the scroll, I am
>   the master of my fate,
> I am the captain of my soul.

Mrs. Schroeder makes the movement with her lips that is too cold to be a smile again.

"See me after school," Mrs. Schroeder says. "Detention."
I snort. The woman looks at me with her cruel eyes.
"Have something to say, dear?"
I suddenly have an idea. It's completely insane, and I'm guaranteed detention. Oh, what the hell? I might as well join her.

> *The caged bird sings*
> *with a fearful trill*

of things unknown
but longed for still

> *and his tune is heard*
> *on the distant hill*

for the caged bird
sings of freedom.

The rest of the class is in shock. The teacher's face is now emotionless.
"Detention for you too, honey."
Adelaide turns around and smiles at me.
"Thanks," she mouths.
"No problem," I whisper.
Her age shouldn't permit it, but Mrs. Schroeder has keen ears.
"Do you want another detention, darling?" she grins wickedly, in full control of her classroom even after what happened mere moments ago.
"No ma'am," Adelaide and I say simultaneously. We try to stifle our laughter. What have I gotten myself into?

Adelaide

THE NEXT PERIOD I HAVE IS ORCHESTRA. IT TURNS OUT TROYE is in orchestra, too. He plays the viola. We have a new teacher this year. I'm going to miss Mrs. Hartman. She was brilliant.

The new teacher is a young guy with thick, hipster-like glasses. His name is Mr. Becker. He asks us to call him Xavier, his first name. Right off the bat we start our playing tests; the incentive is seating. Seating in orchestras is based by skill in each section. The most skilled sit closest to the conductor. Each section is separate: first violins, second violins, violas, cellos, and basses. To some, seats are a big deal. Playing tests determine seating, and they're exactly what they sound like. One must play an excerpt that the teacher assigns. Every violinist plays the same excerpt, every cellist plays the same excerpt, etc. Then, chairs are assigned based on performance.

The basses and cellos have gone. Troye is next. He has a look of utmost concentration on his face. His bow starts to move—no—*glide* across the strings, and I know immediately that he will get first chair. It is exquisite, the sound of the viola. Everyone is entranced. For a second, it is exactly like the auditorium that the pretentious ladies and the buff tattooed guy were in.

When he stops playing, I come to realize that all we have is a stunned orchestra conductor and a bunch of teenage kids. I'd hate being the person who played next.

Xavier speaks. "Well, Adelaide. Mrs. Hartman told me you've been first chair in your section every year. Let's see if you can top that."

Great. I am sitting in the second violin section, and Troye was the last to play in the viola section.

I take a deep breath, put my bow on the strings, and start to play. Everything blurs. I don't see other players with their respective instruments. I don't see anything except the page and my fingers pressing down on the strings. When I finish playing, I'm sort of just sitting there. I am shaken out of my trance not by noise, but by absolute silence. Yet another awkward moment in my awkward life.

I laugh nervously. "I didn't butcher it that badly, did I?"

A boy named Isaac speaks up. "You most definitely topped New Boy."

I chuckle. "Most definitely not."

"Most definitely yes," he responds.

Xavier is the one that speaks this time. "Troye, you're first chair for violas. As for you, Adelaide, we'll just have to see."

The rest of the violins play, and Xavier announces the other chair placements. I am first chair again.

I smile. *Yes!* I think in my head. *Fifth year in a row!*

Times like this, I can't help but be arrogant. I like to think it's self-confidence, but in some classes, I just think, *Wow, I'm completely surrounded by imbeciles.* But hey, I'm rarely proud of myself, so let me have my moment, all right?

We look at our first piece. It is called "Enigma." I look up and see Xavier smiling.

"Cool, huh?" he beams at me.

I grin, the first genuine grin I've had in months. I look back down, eager to see what kind of piece it is. When I first look at a piece of music (i.e., sight-reading), a weird thing happens: I can hear the notes in my head. When I look at this piece, I can hear tragedy and beauty, passion and pain. I hear smooth, enchanting, slurring notes; I hear natural notes that are haunting.

I am thoroughly intrigued, and I can't wait to play it. I go back to the front page to check who wrote this piece. On the top right of the page, in bold black letters is written **Xavier Becker**. I look up yet again. I'm about to speak when a girl named Ana takes the words out of my mouth.

"You wrote this?" she asks.

Xavier nods. "Yeah, just finished it over the summer."

Ana looks apprehensive.

"I got approval from the principal, so it's okay," Xavier adds hurriedly.

Ana nods, and then resumes perusing the pages of music.

I look over, but I'm surprised to see that Ana's music is not similar to mine. "Um . . ." I awkwardly half-raise my hand. "This says—"

"Oh, yes. You, being first in first violin, and 'New Boy' being first in viola, you're playing a duet for us at the RHS Winter Concert."

"Idella," he says, pointing to a petite bassist with silvery-blonde hair, "will be playing with you, Prakash." He nods at a burly Indian boy who is first chair in the cello section.

"Principal Pomeroy has approved this as well."

Principal Kenneth Pomeroy is a big nerd at heart. He has an intimidating form, towering at six foot four. He also has a bulky frame because he was a football player at the age of fourteen. Even so, one could find him in heated discussions with students next to the Performing Arts department of the school, talking about the brand new episodes of pretty much every sci-fi TV show in existence. Most parents find him to be eccentric and odd, so they refrain from talking to him often. He reminds me a bit of *The BFG* by Roald Dahl. He is simply misunderstood.

Speak of the devil—an announcement blares over the speakers.

"Good afternoon, fellow students and staff. We apologize for the interruption. Mr. Pomeroy would like to speak with all seniors in the auditorium. Teachers with the last names S through Z, please send your students down. Other teachers, please wait until your letter is announced."

"So close," Xavier mutters. "I could've kicked you out early if they had started from the beginning of the alphabet."

We wait, and after a little while we are escorted to the auditorium. Mr. Pomeroy is seated on the stage, bathed in the auditorium lights, his receding hairline clearly evident. He clears his throat and taps the mike, drawing attention.

"Today," he says, "we are here to talk about career paths."

You can hear the groan that rises up from the mass of students. The teachers don't notice, though. I think you only detect these things when you're a teenager.

Pomeroy continues. "I know, I know. It sounds pretty boring. But *imagine*. This year, you'll be walking through these halls as a student for the last time. *Ever*. You'll be off doing God knows what. It's your life. Your choices. You can do whatever you love for the rest of your life."

He pauses and looks around, his black eyes gleaming with unexplainable emotion. He then adds, "And I hope to God that the one thing you love isn't weed."

Everyone laughs. If a forty-something-year-old man can make a bunch of disinterested teenagers laugh, anything can happen.

"So, I'd like the room to split into groups containing four people. It's completely up to you; go ahead." He flails his arms around in a dramatic gesture.

We all move into small huddles of people almost immediately. I'm with Troye and two other people, a guy with mocha-colored skin, black hair, and brown eyes, and a pale-skinned girl with platinum blonde hair and startlingly blue eyes. I have no idea what the girl's name is. However, I think the guy's name is Zeke.

"Hi," I say awkwardly.

"Greetings!" the girl says, almost maniacally. She holds her slender hand out for me to shake. "Nice to meet you. My name's Arabella. And you are?"

I shake her hand unadroitly. "Adelaide," I state simply.

"What a lovely name! Nice to meet you!" she repeats brightly.

"You already said that," I mutter quietly, trying not to be rude.

Her lips curve upward. "Oh, there's no problem with that! It's quite healthy to repeat things."

The same sort of ritual happens with Troye.

Zeke waves nonchalantly. "Sorry, my girlfriend is just a *bit* insane."

She gasps and slaps him on the shoulder. "How dare you, Zaidan?" she utters in mock horror. Oh. His name isn't Zeke. My mistake.

"Well, Ara, I have to tell them! You're scaring the poor children!" Zaidan cries dramatically.

It's comical to think about the shortest person in our group calling us children. Zaidan looks five foot five and I am five eight. Troye is definitely more than six feet. Arabella is taller than me, not to mention taller than Zaidan himself. I express this to Zaidan and he laughs like his girlfriend.

"Okay, I won't call you a child," he says vaguely.

I roll my eyes as he turns his attention to Troye.

"Where're you from?" he asks him.

"Uh . . . Florida."

"No, like, way back. Your roots."

"Um . . . I think England?"

"All right." Zaidan ceases speaking with a pensive expression on his face. "Your new name is George Washingturd."

Arabella and I break out into laughter. I laugh just because I am so confused that this situation is getting slightly hysterical to me. Arabella is laughing, most likely, because she knows something about Zaidan and his mannerisms that I don't.

"Wait." Troye squints his eyes. "*What?*"

"Well, Washingturd, George Washington had roots from England because his great-grandfather, John Washington, moved to the US, and Washington reminds me of Washingturd. So, there you go."

"It wasn't acknowledged as the United States back then, so you are technically incorrect. Technically," Arabella states matter-of-factly. I can hear her voice clearly now; she has a deeply American accent with a slightly Southern cadence. She has lost the dreamy demeanor and acts quite normal, which is mildly startling.

Troye looks on in disbelief, while I am thoroughly amused.

"Is this really what you learn in school here in Georgia?" he voices.

This time, Zaidan, Arabella, and I laugh. I nod.

"Absolutely. We learn useless crap that nobody really cares about."

Zaidan gasps. "I care!" he breathes.

I smirk. "Exactly. Nobody."

He gives me a look of unadulterated horror, and I can see why he is dating Arabella.

I point this out to them, and Arabella laughs. "Call me Ara. Or Bella. Or Arabella if you wish, but I don't prefer it. It's quite lengthy."

"All right *Ara*," I say, emphasizing her name. I glance at Zaidan and Troye. They're discussing the pros and cons of some sort of political candidate. I can tell that Zaidan speaks well. He has no clue what he's talking about, yet he still maintains a high level of composure that could faze anyone. He doesn't say much in the discussion, being more of a listener, but what he does say is coherent and intelligent. However, I really don't feel like discussing that particular topic, so I try to pursue a conversation with Ara. I am still getting used to her nickname.

"What about you, Adelaide? Any nicknames? Your name is quite long too," Ara says after I accidently call her Arabella several times throughout bits and pieces of our conversation.

"Um . . . No. Everyone's just called me Adelaide. But my mom does call me Del."

"I might call you Del," she says. She repeats it a couple of times, looking at me with a peculiar expression. "I think I like that," she concludes. "Can I call you Del?"

"Uh, sure," I say uncertainly.

It turns out the grand activity that Pomeroy has planned is only a "get to know you (and your darkest, previously uncompromised secrets)" sort of thing. I learn that Zaidan's favorite color is green and Arabella enjoys tapping her feet to the beat of any music she encounters. I learn that Troye is an only child but has a cousin who has brittle bone disease named Sarah.

The rest of my classes are uneventful. We missed lunch, so we eat in the class right after the assembly is over.

When the final bell of the day marks the time that indicates all tired, grumpy adolescents can leave, and I am very ready to go home and sleep.

Troye

As I'm walking down the hall toward the buses, someone taps me on the shoulder.

"*Follow me*," Adelaide mouths. I nod, confused. We reach an empty corridor, and she says, "The Hawk. Remember?"

I shake my head. "What?"

She sighs. "Schroeder. *The Hawk*. She's got eyes like a hawk. Beady and everything." She gestures to the end of the hall, avoiding my amused grin. "Let's go."

I follow her into the classroom. Mrs. Schroeder is sitting at her desk, evidently immersed in reading *To Kill a Mockingbird*.

I cough quietly, sounding like Professor Umbridge from the Harry Potter series. "*Hem, hem*." I cough again to draw the Hawk's attention.

She looks up from the book with slow, deliberate movements. "Yes?" she says.

"Um . . ." I stutter. "Adelaide and I are here for the detention."

"Oh, right," her face falls. "I nearly forgot about that."

She looks at her watch, a rusty gold wristwatch loosely wrapped around her arm. "I have to go now," she says hesitantly, "so instead of detention, I have an assignment for you. She stands up, grabbing her purse and several other files. "Just . . . uh . . . write a paragraph on what you did in class today and why your behavior was wrong."

I internally groan. If there's anything I hate more than anything, it's writing. I absolutely hate writing, especially about myself.

The Hawk ushers us out the door and then takes off down the hall. I've never seen a woman of that age move so fast. I don't want to miss the bus, so I head down the hall I came from.

"Hey," Adelaide calls. "I can drive you. There's no other seniors on our bus."

I feel my cheeks heat up. I've got a permit, just not a license. Still, the shame of it all makes Adelaide's offer look appealing.

"All right. And it's 'There *are* no other seniors on the bus,'" I say. I pull out my phone and text my parents.

Hey! A friend's dropping me off.

My mom responds immediately.

Okay. Curfew 10.

Got it. I text back.

We walk to the parking lot. Looking amongst the various cars in awe, I see a group of three or four cars that are, well, *amazing*. Two Mercedes, a Cadillac, and a Ferrari. The rest of the cars seem so boring now.

Holy shit, I think. *Wait, that is most definitely not considered shit. Holy perfection. Mortals stand aside.* I would literally get run over with one of those if I could have it afterward.

"Troye!"

I am shaken out of my stupor. Literally. Her hands are on my shoulders.

"Are you okay?"

I nod my head as she lets go of me. We walk toward her car. It's the weirdest car I've ever seen. I have no idea what the hell it is because it is covered in several different fixing materials. Some of it is rusted, some dented, and some scratched. I tear my gaze from the car to meet Adelaide's eyes.

"Bought it used," she says, beaming with pride. "Not a single cent from my parents."

I feign a smile because I don't know how to react. "That's cool."

I assume that she will know I'm lying, but apparently I have picked up the skills of masking my feelings from my mother.

I get in the car. It smells, surprisingly, not of dry sweat, but of lemons and some sort of floral substance. But under that, there is the extremely subtle smell of cigarette smoke. I look at Adelaide, affronted.

"You smoke?" I emphasize my disgust, about to get out of the car and walk home.

She simply looks at me and rolls her eyes. "Used car, remember? Three of my uncles smoked. All of them had heart attacks. I know my limits."

I slump down in relief. "Thank God."

"Indeed . . ." she says absentmindedly, fiddling with the AUX part of her car. A song I don't know comes up, an instrumental piece.

She answers as though she knows exactly what I'm thinking. "I don't like listening to songs with words. They restrict you from interpreting the music as you will. It shouldn't be restrained."

I shake my head in amused disbelief.

"Adelaide, what's your last name?" I question.

She sighs emphatically. "Lillvik-Trumbull."

"*Trunchbull?*" I say, surprised. "Like, the *Matilda*-esque Trunchbull?"

She lets out another sigh. "First off, it's *Trumbull*. Secondly, that isn't the proper use for the suffix '-esque.'"

"Lillvik-Trumbull," I repeat. She nods in confirmation.

"Well then, Adelaide Lillvik-Trumbull, you are *something*."

She momentarily takes her eyes off the road and grins. "I know."

We pass a small huddle of buildings, various shops and restaurants. "Want to get a coffee?"

I shake my head, and she looks affronted. "Don't tell me you don't drink coffee!" she gasps.

I affirm my "unfortunate" dislike with a nod. She puts a hand to her heart.

"What's your last name?" she says.

"Saavedra."

Adelaide gives me a small nod, more of an independent action than a reaction to the name itself.

"That's not as fu—*screwed* up as my name. Not fair at all."

I turn to look at her. "Don't approve of cursing?"

She looks down, which is slightly scary because she is still driving.

"You have to write the paragraph for The Hawk anyway. Come with me."

I sigh. "Fine." I run a hand through my hair tiredly. "I still can't stand coffee, though."

"You've only had Starbucks, haven't you?"

I nod, surprised she has come to this conclusion already. "Yes. I hated it."

"That tells me exactly why you must hate coffee." She smiles in triumph. "In my personal opinion, Starbucks coffee tastes like wet cardboard mixed with the lovely scent of the boys' locker room at school. Let me show you what *real* coffee tastes like."

"Um," I say as she pulls into a parking lot in front of—oh, the irony—Starbucks.

"Adelaide, you do know we're in front of Starbucks, right?"

She rolls her eyes. "I *know*, you dimwit. But we aren't going to Starbucks."

She doesn't bother to clarify what she means. She grabs her backpack and leaves the car, expecting me to follow. I have gotten out of the car, but I am in the same spot, watching her walk toward the brightly lit coffee shop.

She turns around. "You coming?" she asks, exasperated. I nod and follow her. We walk right past Starbucks and into an alleyway.

We reach the metaphorical light at the end of the tunnel and Adelaide looks straight ahead. "There it is," she almost whispers. "My abode."

Her definition of coffee heaven is a dingy-looking bistro. Its sign is so faded that I can't tell what it's named, much like Adelaide's car. Adelaide does that weird mind-reading thing that she does and answers.

"It's called Barakah's Café."

"Interesting," I mutter. "I wonder what that means."

"Blessing," she says immediately. "I'll let Ahmad explain the rest."

We walk in and surprisingly it smells of, well, pure bliss. There is a burly, intimidating-looking guy holding a frying pan inside. I can't help but imagine: one blow and I'd be out cold. He looks at me and snorts.

"I haven't seen a white boy in here since the last time my grandfather actually smiled."

I am slightly confused, but Adelaide smiles warmly. "Hi Ahmad. Good to know that I'm not a boy."

It is Ahmad's turn to chuckle. They talk about things that are only vaguely familiar to me, some not at all, so I just stand there looking to one of them and then the other like this is a tennis match. Finally, Adelaide acknowledges my presence once more.

"Ahmad, tell Troye about Barakah." She says the name endearingly.

Ahmad sits me down, literally. He just awkwardly grabs my shoulders, leads me to a chair, and sort of stuffs me in, which is uncomfortable because I'm six four.

"Barakah was my wife." He looks melancholy, lost in his own emotions, drowning in what William Ernest Henley had phrased as "the bludgeonings of chance." Even though I've only known him for about thirty seconds, I dearly hope that he is, to steal Henley's words again, "unbowed."

Ahmad tells me about his spouse, a gentle woman who rarely raised her voice. She had some sort of paralysis consuming her body. She eventually became bedridden. The one thing that she did was to ask the girl living next door to bring her coffee. It was the highlight of her day, and she would always have a laptop with her. She was strangely obsessed with coffee itself, and was often doing ostensibly important research at all hours of the day.

After she passed away, Ahmad decided he would run a café in her honor. He wanted to be an engineer of some sort, but he loved his wife much more than his ambitions.

After Ahmad finishes telling me—a person he has never seen before—his life story, there is a bittersweet silence, the air filled with emotions. If I were my mother, I would run from here as quickly as I could. "Too many emotions," she would've said. But, fortunately, I am not.

I sit in silence, and as I would expect, Adelaide shatters it.

"Ahmad, can you make us some coffee? This boy needs enlightenment."

Ahmad looks extremely uncomfortable, shaking his head and muttering something about modern teenagers.

While waiting for the coffee, we look at Ahmad and, surprisingly, Ahmad is a swan in the open kitchen. His movements are graceful even though he looks ill at ease.

When he serves it, I have to admit, it smells fragrant and unexplainable. As I lean the cup toward my mouth, I see Adelaide gazing at me intensely, studying my every move. I close my eyes and take a sip.

Oh. God*damn*. The kick that coffee gives you excites the taste buds, forcing you to get used to its strong flavor. I could die a happy man right now. I set the cup down. Adelaide's lips are curled into an I-told-you-so smile.

"That was amazing," I breathe. Then I raise the cup back to my lips and drain it. "Where has this been all my life?"

"Better latte than never," Adelaide smirks.

I mirror her expression. "Thanks, Adelaide, for espresso-ing yourself."

"All right, to work," she says when our laughter fades. She takes out a piece of paper, a red pen, and starts to write.

"Adelaide, you know you're writing with a red pen, right?" I say.

Without looking up, she answers me. "I know. Teachers use red pen. That's why I use red pen. I only do it to teachers I particularly dislike."

"Isn't that a bit too irritating?"

She shrugs her shoulders. "They sabotage my educational experience. Why not bother them a bit without any serious repercussions?"

I laugh. "That's actually quite a pathetic attempt. Please try harder."

"You'll see," she says. The conversation ceases from there. I sigh, and then start writing my paragraph.

"Dear Mrs. Schroeder,

"I apologize for my atrocious behavior in class today. I was completely out of line to disrupt the order in your classroom . . . and more crap that I don't actually mean."

I read my paragraph out loud to Adelaide, who looks up lazily in boredom. Then her face lights up.

"My turn," she whispers. Then, picking up her paper, she clears her throat and starts to read.

"Dear Mrs. Schroeder (or authoritarian dictator),

"I sincerely apologize for the expression of my personal beliefs and poetic knowledge in your class. I didn't realize that these days, students weren't allowed to express their beliefs in a creative, entertaining way to clarify how they truly feel. From now on, I promise I will be a mindless monotonous machine produced by the American public school system. I promise not to show an active imagination or any difference from the average student. I look forward to being manufactured by you.

"Best Wishes,

"Adelaide Lillvik-Trumbull."

"That's going to piss The Hawk off," I state, not quite sure what to say.

Adelaide beams. "I know. That was the point."

"Not that I would mind, of course," I add quickly. "The way she says 'darling' or 'honey.' It sounds like assault."

Adelaide chuckles. "I know. *Troye Saavedra, aged seventeen, verbally assaulted by 'The Hawk' Schroeder.* What a tragic incident. It would make headlines."

I shudder. "Don't give me that mental image. It's disturbing."

"Anyway," she shakes her head with amusement. "Let's go."

She gets up and thanks Ahmad.

"No problem!" he says. "Next time, bring the white boy again!"

She drops me home, where I am left to process all that has happened today.

Weeks pass by. Fall slips into winter. Used to being in rather warm temperatures, I hate the cold—and *damn*, is it cold. There was only one, no—two problems. One: Schroeder. We still have to deal with the usual monotonous ideals, although now she looks considerably older. Her hair is graying rapidly, and her skin gets more prunish day by day. She has become more aggressive, not physically, but in her daily interaction.

Unfortunately, the same is happening to my mother, minus the prune part, which brings me to number two. Her eyes are becoming dimmer and dimmer, and wrinkles have started to appear on her face. About two weeks ago, she took a new job under a strict boss, slaving in front of a computer all day, as her company feels software engineers should. She works long hours and returns home late at night. Additionally, she has started a charity for the less fortunate all over America. As a result, as soon as she returns home, she pours over paperwork and makes several important phone calls.

On this particular day, she is fulfilling her self-inflicted duties in the paperwork department when I get home.

"Good to see you," I say. "How was your day?"

She remains silent. I know she can hear me. "Mom," I say again a bit louder. "Mom?" She doesn't respond again.

My entire life I have been raised as some peculiar burden on both my parents. My mother never gave me a second glance when I was younger, and I guess that still applies today. I remember once, when I was in kindergarten, the teacher told us to make a picture of our family. So I did. I worked for an hour on the most fabulous drawing I had ever made in the entire lifespan I lived so far. I gave it to my mother. She smiled at me for about a second, snatched the drawing, and resumed her work immediately.

Long story short: the next day, I found my art in the garbage.

I lose my temper simply because of her unsatisfying silence.

"Mom," I hiss. "I know you're being a *brilliant* person to *tons* of families, but for *once*, can you take care of your own?"

My mom freezes midway through a sentence.

"Troye James Saavedra, you will apologize this instant," she said emotionlessly, but she still doesn't look up.

I laugh bitterly. "Or what, Mom? Are you going to throw my drawing away again?" I don't stay in her sight long enough to gauge her reaction.

I go upstairs to my still-unpainted room. I barely glance at anything, my whole body being consumed with figurative fire, churning with rage. I storm into my closet and pack one set of clothes. There's only one place I can go: Zaidan's. He'll know what to make of this.

His home is about half an hour away by foot. I walk there under stormy clouds. I have always loved this mysterious, enigmatic weather. It sets the mood where anything can happen. It has the whole feeling of epiphanic, tragic allure. When I finally reach Zaidan's red brick home, my feet are numb from the cold. Sighing, I ring the doorbell.

Zaidan's father opens the door. He is an introvert, an engineer with graying hair and bad posture. He scans me for a second, taking in my disheveled appearance, and then turns to face the staircase.

"Zaidan, your friend is here!" he shouts. Afterward, he promptly walks away and into the depths of their enormous home.

Zaidan reaches the door, holding a small child in his arms: his little sister, Persephone. I thought Zaidan's entire family's names must be extravagantly eloquent. But previously, when I had asked Zaidan about his parents' names, he said simply and honestly, "Ann and Dean." Zaidan looks me up and down and makes an accurate assessment.

"You look like shit, Washingturd. Get in."

The Markley home is a maze; it has about six stories and a gigantic backyard. Zaidan leads me down an unrecognizable hallway and I somehow end up in his room. His room is odd, the walls painted black (except one, which is gray), yet all the furniture is shockingly white. On his walls, there is an assortment of video game posters, debate team medals, and an entire corner full of movie tickets pinned to a corkboard. The oddest and coolest thing, though, is his fireplace, right next to a gigantic circular window that has a sort of built-in bench next to it.

"Wait here." Zaidan treads out of the door and into the maze.

I don't know what to do, so I just sit on the edge of his bed, wondering what the hell I'm doing with my life.

When he returns, he's carrying a bright-pink sleeping bag with flowers on it. Looking at my grimace, he retorts amusedly, "It's this or nothing at all. It's Ophelia's, from when she was twelve."

Ophelia is Zaidan's older sister, an overachiever. She took her A-levels and the SAT in her junior year. She hated peculiar names. In fact, when she had reached high school she told everyone to call her Sophie. As soon as she graduated she was snatched up by some prestigious school in the United Kingdom.

Zaidan hasn't heard from her since then, other than a couple of emails. He had also gotten one from a random lady, presumably Ophelia's mother-in-law, because it had announced Ophelia's wedding. However, it was definitely *not* an invitation. By the time the rest of the Markley family found out about the wedding, Ophelia Markley had become Sophie Robertson. Reluctantly, I pick up the bag and set it on the ground next to Zaidan's bed.

"Hey, why can't I sleep in your bed too? It's massive!" I say. I, unlike some guys, have no problem sharing a bed with the same gender. To me, it is trivial.

Zaidan rolls his eyes. "Firstly, I'm as straight as a ruler, and secondly, I have a girlfriend to share it with. She, by the way, is coming over with Adelaide."

I grimace. "You had to invite them?"

The shorter boy grins. "Couldn't resist."

Shortly after that conversation, I hear the doorbell ring. It has a deep resonance, reverberating throughout the house. It reminds me of the clock in Edgar Allan Poe's *The Masque of Red Death*—creepy.

When the two other teenagers enter the room, I am huddled into Ophelia's flowery sleeping bag. Adelaide takes one look at me and laughs.

"Nice sleeping bag; was it your grandmother's?" she quips.

"Ha. Bloody. Ha." I mutter obscenities under my breath.

She turns to Zaidan. "I forgot a sleeping bag; can you get me one?"

Zaidan nods swiftly and walks out of the room. He returns almost immediately with a navy-blue sleeping bag with a grayish interior.

I look down at mine. "I thought you said you didn't have another one!" I protest.

"Slipped my mind," he remarks slyly.

I turn to Adelaide.

"Please," I say.

She looks at me with faux innocence, batting her eyelids too many times. "Please, what?"

I groan. "Can we *please* switch sleeping bags?"

She smirks, her eyes glinting mischievously. She pretends to think about the idea of giving me her bag, then comes to a predestined conclusion.

"No thanks," she says, the corners of her mouth turning upward.

"Adelaide, please," I beg, trying to stare into the depths of her brown eyes.

Her decision remains unchanged.

"Dammit," I mutter under my breath. I then raise my voice and complain. "Why is it *me* that gets stuck with the flowery spawn of Satan?"

We don't do much that night. I end up telling them about the stress, the anxiety, my mother. I tell them about my utter brokenness. I let out everything I have held back from anyone I have ever met.

I hadn't planned to say any of this, but looking at the trio's encouraging smiles, and the bright, understanding eyes, every backwater thought centered around every problem I have had in my life gushes from my mouth.

They don't react badly when I tell them any of my vile resentments against people I interacted with regularly, although

I can see Ara wince when she hears that my parents fight often. She pulls her sleeve down and shivers, seemingly cold.

"What about?" she asks.

"I'd rather not say." My fingernails form small indents in the center of my palm.

"I understand," she replies. "Now go on; tell us more."

My father is an intriguing personality. He doesn't care what anyone thinks. I think he used to. He has an array of sharp jibes at his disposal, and he is disgustingly blunt about how he feels.

Regardless of the more recent deterioration of my parents' marriage, I had still heard stories about what they used to be. My father was as charming as an unemployed college graduate could get, and it was no wonder that he chose my mother to be his confidante, as she was his counterpart: just as suave and collected. What happened along the road of solidarity that lead to widespread cracks, I have no idea.

It is painful to talk about my parents, but I feel like the three people sitting in front of me deserve to know about my dad, and everything in my old life. It's the closest they can come to understanding my feelings.

The only thing left to do is go to bed. Ara crawls to the other side of Zaidan's bed and is instantly asleep. Adelaide sets her sleeping bag a couple of feet away from mine.

The sleeping bag is too hot to sleep in, as I am right next to the fireplace, so I settle on top. I ponder the ridiculous things that Adelaide tells me about "the tragically delicate system of the fatalistically bittersweet world and its seemingly timeless facade" on our weekly coffee trips.

My first thought is this: she *has* to stop using that many complex words in a single sentence. My second is that her insanity might be starting to make sense. Or my sanity is giving way to a whole new world of psychotic possibilities. Same thing, really.

When I wake up, it's just before sunrise. After a few seconds of bleary disorientation, I immediately notice that I am wrapped around a navy-blue sleeping bag. Confused as to where my flowery mess of a sleeping bag went, I sit up. I look to my left and see Adelaide sitting on the window bench, sitting knees up, the flowery spawn of Satan bunched up around her feet.

She looks over when she hears me get up. "Hi," she whispers. She pats the spot next to her. I get up groggily and stagger over.

"What's with the change?" I say nonchalantly, gesturing to the sleeping bags. Adelaide shrugs.

"I was the last one to fall asleep. You looked a bit pathetic with your floral disaster and all. I felt bad."

I gasp. "The impermeable Adelaide Lillvik-Trumbull has *emotions*? *What a surprise!*" Adelaide slaps my arm. Nevertheless she is chuckling. I gasp even louder. "*And she resorts to physical abuse! My word!*"

She giggles. "My word?" She scrunches up her nose. "That sounds like you're in a Latino soap opera."

I try to sound as dramatic as I possibly can. "*And now you're stereotyping the Latin American races! Shame on you, wicked girl!*"

Adelaide shakes her head as if utterly disappointed in me. "I bet that a super-rich Latina actress wouldn't take offense." There is a pause. "And if she does, she can cry into her hundred-dollar bills. Or whatever currency she's paid in."

She lets out a low, hearty laugh. Thankfully, it doesn't wake up the other two.

Arabella, whose legs are currently tangled with Zaidan's, shifts a bit in her sleep, but that's it.

Zaidan, who remains in his snoring state, doesn't move an inch.

"You know what would make this even better?" I shake my head and she responds, "A cup of coffee."

I smile. "Well, I'm not expecting Ahmad to jump out of a random closet." I feign to ponder this idea. "Or . . . should I expect it?"

Adelaide nods, chortling. She tentatively puts her feet on the midnight-oak floor. She puts a finger to her lips and tiptoes out of the room. I hesitantly follow her.

When we are both outside and Zaidan's bedroom door is shut, she says, "C'mon. We're going to make some coffee."

"How do you know where the kitchen is?" I say, gesturing to the sheer size of the house.

"That's a story you'll hear in a minute," she states plainly, not caring to elaborate further. I do notice, however, a light shade of crimson washing across her cheeks, not necessarily blush. I decide to leave it for now. I follow her through this tunnellike hall, except the walls have a surplus of large windows on both sides. The view is an ornate, impeccable garden, and with the breathtaking sunrise, the scenery looks magnificent. The vividly red-orange rays emitting from the shimmering orb of pure flames soak into my pale skin, making me feel renewed. I am immersed both in my own thoughts and the warm feeling of liquid sunlight washing over me. It is only when Adelaide puts her hand on my shoulder, a melancholy curtain draped across her bright eyes, that I remember I am standing in the middle of a hallway in a home, and not a faraway galaxy that only I reside in.

"We can see the sunrise from the kitchen, too. There's a window in there." She grips my right arm with her hand and steers me to a room all the way at the end of the hall. It's just as stylish as the rest of the house: whitewashed walls that look a bit too perfect and dark furniture with intricate designs. I unintentionally shudder.

Adelaide speaks with her eyes still fixed on the horizon. "I know. It used to be a lot . . . warmer."

I look at her with concern. "How do you know this, Adelaide?"

She doesn't say anything until her coffee has been drained. She then takes a seat next to me.

She smiles wistfully. I don't like it at all. She looks like what Adelaide Lillvik-Trumbull, the unmitigated, unadulterated embodiment of *something*, can't possibly be: upset. The girl that I know to be so level-headed and strong has smacked me across the face without lifting a finger. She has proven to me that she is just a human, something that I have been forgetting lately.

"This coffee is like déjà-brew."

We both chuckle and then fall back into silence.

Minutes later, Adelaide's voice pierces the silence. "You want to know, right?" Her words startle me.

"What?" I say.

"You know . . . the house thing."

I blink, confused, then realize what she's talking about. "Oh, yeah, if you want."

She sighs, obviously hesitating. "When I moved here from Los Angeles, my family had a really cool house. But when my dad left, he took most of the money, left me with my mom, and she started struggling. A lot." I am surprised that her parents were divorced, but I let her continue. I hate interrupting people, and I'm sure they hate it too. "We had to sell the house and move into the one we live in now." She sighs again. "And you guessed it: my mom sold it to Zaidan's parents. This used to be my house."

I'm not really surprised. "Your parents are divorced?" I say tentatively.

She nods, not looking uncomfortable at all. "I don't hate him though."

I'm confused (*Yet* again; *way to go, Troye!* I think to myself).

"Can you explain that? Just a bit befuddled."

"He's a good person. You know, pays taxes, took care of me, as far as that can go when you don't live with your kid. But, you know, love is love. He couldn't resist falling in love with someone who just didn't happen to be my mom. He never cheated on my mom. He just, no matter how hard he tried—" Adelaide's voice cracks a little bit, and she blinks her eyes furiously. "He couldn't stay in love with her," she whispers, her voice hoarse.

I don't say anything. This isn't one of those times when you should. We sit enveloped in the silence that fills every corner of the room. We allow it to cover us in artificial comfort, letting us know that nothing but it itself could cease the tension. But screw it. Silence is a lie, the mere absence of sound. And because I am so Troye-ish (normal, except perhaps that I am exceedingly great at being a Washingturd), and because Adelaide is so Adelaide-ish, so good at being *something*, I have to shatter the silence.

"Adelaide—"

"*Shh*," she says, not even looking at me.

"What?"

She sighs, irritated, but explains anyway. "Our adversary is silence."

I shake my head. "But if our adversary is silence, shouldn't we speak louder?"

"No." She explains this to me as if I were two. "Some random wise person, I forget, said, 'Don't fight fire with fire.' But there are some days when you just need to blowtorch everything."

"But still—"

"Shh," she repeats. "Silence may be our adversary, but its adversary is our silence."

And that is how we watch the sun rise. Our feet are propped up on Mrs. Markley's very expensive mahogany dinner table, and we sip coffee, not a word exchanged once.

When Zaidan and Arabella arrive hand-in-hand, they are accompanied by a joyful-looking woman who I assume to be Mrs. Markley.

"Three seconds to get your feet off the table," Zaidan whispers to us, grinning.

"Seriously, she's going to kill you."

We do as we are told.

"Morning!" the woman says cheerily. She looks at Adelaide and I with an amused expression. "If you two want to make out or something, please go outside. Just letting you know." She turns the stove on, and faces Arabella and Zaidan. "That goes for you too."

Zaidan's mom makes me feel uncomfortable and comfortable simultaneously. It's a weird feeling, but I like it I guess. She's so blunt about everything that it makes me feel like she never censored around her kids when they were young, exposing them to the real world early on.

The smell of waffles and fresh fruit fills the air quickly. "Thank you Mrs. Markley," Adelaide and I say simultaneously.

She shrugs off the compliments we give her about the food. "And please, call me Ann," she adds.

And obviously, we respond with, "Okay, Mrs. Markley."

We laugh and eat and talk. I am filled with the euphoria of being cared about. Adelaide. Zaidan. Arabella. Even Mrs. Markley. It is nice to be acknowledged as an equal, or even acknowledged at all, really.

"All right, guys, I need to head to work."

"Oh, okay," Adelaide says. "What do you do?"

"Oh, I just cook, sweetie. Nothing much."

Zaidan nearly spits out his OJ.

"Mom, you're the *executive chef* at *your own restaurant*."

"Ooh, what's it called?" Adelaide questions.

"Achilles Steakhouse."

She looks surprised. "I've been there! Amazing food!"

Mrs. Markley beams. "I'm glad you like it. You should stop by again one day."

Adelaide mirrors her expression. "I most definitely will."

The older woman clears up some dishes and leaves. All is well. Zaidan puts his feet on the table and his arm around Arabella. "Ah, a fine Saturday morning."

In that moment, I know something is wrong because one, Arabella pushes off Zaidan's arm; two, her body becomes rigid, and she gets up immediately; and three, she is sobbing.

Adelaide

ZAIDAN IS THE FIRST TO REACT. IN AN INSTANT, HE IS RIGHT beside her, gripping her hand reassuringly. "What's wrong, Ara?"

She sniffles. "It's Saturday. I had a recital today."

"What does she play?" I whisper to Zaidan.

"Nothing anymore, as far as I know."

I turn my attention to Ara. "Which recital? Was it yours?"

Ara shakes her head. "It was for Logan. My little brother. He plays piano. He's a prodigy." Her knees hit the ground with a sickening thump, but nothing is broken.

"I promised. I promised I'd come. Why do I always have to screw up everything?" She cries even harder.

When you get closer and closer to someone, you hit pockets of their own doubts, insecurities, and negative experiences. I think I have just witnessed Arabella come to a screeching halt, standing at the foot of her personal hell: herself. She thinks we can't hear her when she says to herself, "Why am I such a fuck-up?"

There are probably things I don't know about Ara, secrets that have never seen the light of day. But for some reason, I sit next to her and breathe to myself, "Don't worry, Ara. We all are."

After we drop Ara home via Zaidan's car, we all visit her at least twice a week. Zaidan seems to get paler every time he returns from her home. Troye has to have his mom drop him off as he hasn't tested for his license yet. He looks more frustrated than usual.

Life goes on, the only option it has other than to exterminate itself.

Arabella's condition is getting worse. Whenever I visit, she is huddled under a layer of musty blankets and tissues. The same scenario is laid out before me today. I greet her, then go to her bathroom. I pick up the bloodstained razors and dispose of them, putting them in places where she can't find them anymore. I look in her typical hiding places: under the sink, the back of her medicine cabinet, her closet. She doesn't even look up once. Zaidan doesn't know about this part of her dilemma; he simply sits on a stool and looks at her.

I sit and talk to her, bandaging her arms. She makes no attempt to speak back. I don't know why she takes her brother's recital to heart. When I spoke to Logan, the scraggly ten-year-old boy with glasses, he seemed okay with the fact that she had missed it. I assume that it was the last step off the cliff, the tight embrace of the fall, the one last thing that pushed her over the edge.

It's a shame. It isn't a matter of shame that she is upset to this extent. It is a shame that society is proud of uplifting youth, yet they can't support the ones who are actually having issues. They don't see the silent sobs, the quiet pain. They don't see the dripping of blood, the guilty satisfaction of the youth who have been taught to loathe their own skin.

And it is sad.

I get a text, jolting me out of my thoughts.

Wanna head for coffee at Barakah's? Troye asks.

I'm with Ara, I text back.

"If it's Troye, go," says Ara. Her voice is raspy from disuse. Ara looks at me with hollow eyes. This is the first time that I have properly seen her eyes in two weeks. "Ara!" I say, a bit too excited. Then I deflate a bit. "Um . . . You okay?"

"*Litost*," she says promptly.

"I'm sorry, what?" I say.

"Litost," she repeats. "It's Czech."

I nod my head as an indication for her to elaborate.

She continues. "It means, and I quote from the ever-reliable Internet, 'a state of torment created by the sudden sight of one's own misery.' Quite fitting, don't you think?"

"Is it Zaidan?" I question.

She shakes her head tearily. "No, it's just—quite—I feel stupid saying this, but, it's quite *overwhelming*. I think I just need some time to figure out what I'm doing with my life. It's just all this stress and panic building up after years. It hurts. Pretty badly."

It's like she's forcing the words out of her mouth. I can understand the feeling of not being able to express yourself like you intend to.

I nod. "Oh, I understand. It's perfectly okay. I'll be here as long as you'd like me to be here."

She reaches out and grabs my wrist. "No." She looks into my eyes with a meaningful look, although I'm not quite sure what it means yet. "Go meet him."

I stand shakily and give Ara a tentative hug. "Don't do anything stupid," I whisper in her ear.

"I won't." Her lips form the words shakily. *I'll try*, her eyes seem to say.

I hope to God that that is enough.

What the small world of high school, and perhaps the rest of the world, needs to understand is that the world is more complex than we actually think. It is so complex that its levels of complexity vary. Take, for example, several different adversaries that people face in their lives. They can be extremely simple for one person to solve, but nearly impossible for someone else. This is how the world is, and I can appreciate that.

When I arrive at the Starbucks parking lot, I am surprised to find that Troye is not alone. I can see him first, with his plaid shirt with the sleeves rolled up and his signature black Converses, leaning against Zaidan's car. His light-brown hair is mussed; it looks like he just woke up. He is accompanied by a slouching form in the passenger seat: Zaidan. Troye sees me but doesn't smile. He simply shrugs his shoulders and gestures to Zaidan. The brown-eyed boy in question is hunched over, back shaking. Next to him, in the cupholder, is an untouched mug of coffee.

Troye looks slightly desperate. "*Help*," he mouths.

I stand next to him. "What happened?" I whisper, my voice low.

He shrugs. "I don't know what happened. We were over at my house, and he just kinda—" He makes a spectacular sort of gesture indicating that Zaidan got this way all of his own accord. I shut him up, give him a reassuring look, and sit in the driver's seat.

"*Get in the back,*" I mouth to Troye.

He obliges, and I start the car, the engine coughing itself to life.

Zaidan's head snaps up, which is unfortunate because he is still hunched over. His head hits the bottom of the dashboard. He sits up shakily, rubbing his head.

"Ow!" he complains. "What the hell are you doing?"

"Shut up, Zaidan," I laugh. "We're going camping." I take a sip of his coffee, keeping my eyes on the road.

Zaidan turns to Troye when I pull out of the parking space.

"Troye, your girlfriend's insane."

I can't see Troye's face, but I assume it's red, like it usually is when he's flustered. "She's not my girlfriend," he mutters.

I laugh a bit maniacally and turn around to face him. (I know, I know, horrible driving etiquette, but it was only for a second.)

"You wish, Saavedra."

The last thing I see before I turn around is his face gleaming with some sort of emotion.

"Definitely not, Lillvik-Trumbull."

I grin, gripping the steering wheel.

"Dammit," I hear him whisper. "Lillvik-Trumbull doesn't have the same effect as Saavedra."

I am thoroughly amused.

"Where are we camping anyway?" Zaidan asks, breaking the sudden awkwardness of the conversation.

I stop the car at my home. I get out immediately. "Give me five minutes," I say, rushing my words. "Oh, and"—I grab the car key—"you can't leave."

Troye rolls his eyes. "Like we were actually going to go anywhere, Adelaide."

I ignore his statement. "Oh, and you—" I point to Troye. "Get some stuff. You know, for sleeping."

Troye smirks. "Wow, what an excellent choice of vocabulary. Your instructions are duly noted."

I don't have time to come up with a sarcastic remark, so instead I sprint inside and pack a bag full of clothes, grab a sleeping bag, and write a note to my mom explaining why I won't be returning home.

When I go back outside, Zaidan is sitting stiffly in the front and Troye is lounged in the backseat, his long legs spread over the other two seats.

"You didn't respond to me before you got out of the car," Troye gasps in mock horror at this notion. He should wipe that smirk off his face before I smack him.

"*L'esprit de l'escalier*," I say.

"I take Spanish," Troye says.

"I'm fluent in witty remarks," Zaidan adds. "I don't need French."

I roll my eyes. "It's the act of thinking of a witty comeback after it's too late to actually say it. French is actually quite useful. Zaidan, next stop, your house."

"No need," he says. "I've already got stuff in the trunk. Always do."

"Okay?" I say hesitantly.

He changes the topic rapidly, wrapping his hands around the now cold cup of coffee.

"Again, may I ask, where are we going to camp?"

It is my turn to smirk. "The Tower."

I can hear the sharp intake of breath. He looks not so much mortified, but confused.

"Not . . . the Tower? Like the actual Tower?"

"I'm sorry," Troye says, putting his hand on the head of the passenger seat. "But what's the—"

"Highest tower of Rookwood High School. Nobody ever goes there. Every year, the current seniors of the year tell the freshman about the Tower. In the first year that Rookwood High School was established, a student tried to jump off."

Zaidan tries to remain solemn, but I can see an extremely subtle smirk playing on his lips.

"What happened to him?" Troye looks a bit concerned.

I can't stand it anymore. I laugh. "He fell. But onto a balcony about ten feet below. It was a prank."

Troye looks relieved. Zaidan turns to me.

"But Adelaide, it's way too far up; you have to climb a ton of stairs. There's also the fact that *we have to break into the school to reach it*, and that, Adelaide, is something we call *illegal*."

I, for probably the millionth time in my life, roll my eyes.

"Oh shut up, you pompous—sarcastic—*swine*." In between each of the last three words, I hit Zaidan on the arm with my hand.

"Ouch, jeez, Adelaide, that really hurt." He morphs his face into an affected somber expression and puts a hand on his chest. "And so does my heart."

I hit him again. "Shut up, and let me drive." I pronounce every word slowly.

He doesn't respond, which is wise.

When we reach Rookwood High, some of the lights are still on as a surprisingly significant amount of teachers are still in the building (judging by the number of cars parked outside).

"Text Ara. Tell her where we're going."

The words slip out of my mouth, waiting for no one. Zaidan looks slightly perturbed. "What do you mean?"

"She deserves to know. And if she would like to join, she is more than welcome."

The shorter boy laughs bitterly in response. It's the worst sound I have ever heard in my entire life—sharp, cold, and entirely un-Zaidanish. The chuckling boy that I met on the day of the Career Path lecture is gone. He has been replaced by a shell of what he used to be.

"I just . . . I don't want her to see me like this." He gestures to himself awkwardly. Now I can see him better.

His eyes are bloodshot. He looks like he hasn't slept in days. It breaks my heart to see him like this. It's the worst thing in the world. I look back at Troye, and his expression matches mine, although he has another emotion swirling in his eyes. Is it . . . could it really be . . . familiarity? But then I realize that he should be used to it, comforting someone he cares for. *His mother.* Troye must feel like crap right now. And it sucks. It really does.

"I mean, I know the ladies love looking at me, but not right now." Zaidan has to crack a joke, even when his voice is grainy and strained. I can't help but laugh. It feels good to laugh.

"Must you make a joke at this moment? It was getting so dramatic and you ruined it," I say.

Zaidan, grins, his chapped lips stretching into a smile. I look back again and Troye still looks a bit troubled. Then, seeing that I am looking at him, he gives me a weak smile.

"I'm okay," he mouths.

"I wish you were," I say, resulting in a startled look from him and a knowing stare from me. We stay like that for about three seconds before I remember that Zaidan is in the car.

"Sorry," I say briskly, opening the door to the car and getting out, brushing nonexistent dirt off my jeans. "Unnecessary awkward tension."

I don't know if my ears are failing me, but I swear I hear Zaidan mutter, "In more ways than one." I pretend not to hear, as it is extremely convenient as of now.

We walk up to the front of the school and I say, "Right, now how are we going to get in?"

Troye steps forward and pulls open the front door. "How about from here?" he suggests, a smirk on his face.

"Oh, shut up."

We walk in silence, the buzz of adrenaline crackling in the air around us. It's a euphoric feeling, walking with sleeping bags in hand, the odd beauty of an empty school before us. We have almost reached the stairs for the Tower. All we must do is pass the gym. But even before we get there, I can hear the sound of the Armageddon: the slamming of basketballs in the gym, a place I've never voluntarily been. The basketball team has practice today. We're screwed. As if right on time, a gruff voice sounds from the door. Coach Di Masi, a large fellow who is the kind of person who picks favorites just to make other kids feel bad, is towering over two of us (he can't tower over Troye because Troye is taller than him), eying our sleeping bags.

"What're you kids doing here at this time of the night?"

"We, uh . . ." I rack my brain for some good excuses. "We—"

"Wearegoingtothetower," Troye mumbles. His face is white, his hands clammy and shaky. I take it he doesn't do well under pressure. The lanky boy turns into a cowering child. If we weren't about to potentially get kicked out, I might have laughed. *Who knew, the tallest, most intimidating of all of us is the most scared?*

"Excuse me, son?"

I roll my eyes internally. *Do all gruff gym teachers call people "son"?* Troye, fear apparent in his eyes, clears his throat.

"*Hem. Hem.* We're going to the Tower." His voice is small, but Di Masi's voice is scarily loud.

"Are you kids *insane*? It's the middle of winter! It's too dangerous! And never mind that, how did you get into the school? Did a teacher let you in? You three will get the highest punishment close to expulsion, I'll make sure of it! You don't have permission, and I most certainly will not authorize it!"

We have no time to react and nothing to say to defend ourselves, but even Di Masi jumps when the four of us hear a smooth, familiar voice.

"Is there an issue with my students, Florence?" Xavier, holding a cello that is missing a string, has appeared from almost nowhere.

I can hear Zaidan snort. "*Florence?*" he mouths. Then, he leans closer, and his voice slithers to my ears, barely audible. "Can you imagine how much his parents loved him, naming him Florence, of all things?" I have to hold in my laughter, my sides shaking painfully from the effort. But the need to laugh dies a bit when *Florence* glares at me, his eyes full of poison.

"I'm just about to punish these hooligans. They've been breaking and entering and—"

"Excuse me," Zaidan straightens his back to reach his full height, which, unfortunately for him, isn't that much taller. "We walked in through the front door."

"But that's it, boy!" Di Masi says, shaking an accusatory finger at him. "Why did you get in in the first place? I will have no ruffians tarnishing the sanctity of this school!"

"Florence, please, calm down." Xavier looks over at us, his eyes bright and kind. "These students, they're here as per my request. They're here to, uh, practice a piece of music." Di Masi isn't appeased.

"Then why do they have sleeping bags? And that boy . . ." he points to Troye, "told me they were going to the Tower."

"Ah, well you see," Xavier reasons, not hesitating, "they are also going to be going to the Tower for . . . an assignment for orchestra. I can't give you the details. They were just going to come to the orchestra room for a bit, and then head on up."

Di Masi looks highly irritated, but he nods. "I'll take your word for it, *Xavier*."

He strides back into the gym. We hear the squeaking of shoes and basketballs cease, and a collective groan as the coach tells them to begin the infamous exercise known as "suicides."

I can't help but sigh in relief. I look at Xavier and say thank you, as do the other boys.

"No problem. You guys can get on with whatever the hell—*sorry*, that wasn't appropriate teacher conduct." He stands up straight. "You three beloved, respected students of the grand institution that is known as Rookwood High School may continue your diligent, enigmatic work, in whatever field that may be."

He is about to usher us away, but then, as I had silently predicted moments before, Di Masi walks out of the gym yet again, to our dismay. He wears an evil grin. "Xavier, I couldn't help but overhear—"

"We'll be going now," Xavier interrupts quickly, completely ignoring him. "We've got work to do."

He doesn't wait for Di Masi to answer, but instead strides away. We, the willingly obedient pupils, follow our teacher, imitating his affected, pretentious, and gliding way of walking. I give backward glances to see if the coach is gone already. But there he is, standing a foot away from the entrance of the gym, watching us walk all the way to the orchestra room. When I walk into the dimly lit room, glowing only with a couple of lamps that reflect off of the mahogany-colored instruments, I hear Zaidan let out a laugh of triumph. "*Florence* tripped in the doorway and fell on his ass."

The rest of us, stifling laughter, decide to ignore his statement altogether.

"I'm just going to pretend I didn't hear that," Xavier says vaguely, a shadow of a smile adorned on his face.

"Well, now that you're here, why don't you play "Enigma" for this young fellow? You need the practice," Xavier suggests.

Troye turns white. I mean, whiter than he already is. I shrug my shoulders. Why not? "I'd love to," I say.

Troye

I CAN'T SAY THAT I'M NOT NERVOUS. I'M PRACTICALLY SHAKING. I have practiced this piece with Adelaide approximately once. I feel myself grabbing the slender neck of my ostensibly archaic viola. Why am I tightening my bow? Why am I tuning my viola? Oh okay, now I'm grabbing my music. Just *brilliant*. With the expansive crowd of two people watching us, I feel snakes in my stomach, as butterflies aren't as manly.

I look at Adelaide. "Ready?" I say.

"Ready," she replies.

We commence playing. I realize how much I enjoy playing an instrument, the satisfaction of sliding a horsehair bow across four strings. It is an amazingly pleasurable feeling, the realization of the music you make simply by being decently coordinated and collected. I understand that all that is preventing me from playing is myself, and I won't let myself do that—not this time. I allow the music to fill the sound around me, covering up the tension in the room. It feels exceedingly okay to be here. I always enjoy listening to music, no matter who is playing it, because it is a beautiful thing.

When we finish, there is a comfortable silence, one that isn't our adversary.

"You have a couple of high notes that definitely need some work, and some other things that we'll discuss later, but, overall, excellent." Xavier nods. "Good job, guys."

Zaidan speaks up. "You two are going to have some pretty talented kids. That was brilliant."

"Thanks," I say, placing my bow into my viola case. "All right, let's get to the Tower."

"Yes!" Zaidan jumps in anticipation, looking almost comical, his eyes wide and gleaming with delight.

We pick up our belongings, bid adieu to Xavier, and head out of the room. With the stealth and speed of ninjas who have just set off a mass amount of alarms, we clumsily run to a brick archway at the end of the hall—the entrance to the Tower. Even before we open the glass door, I can already feel the cold creeping up my spine. This will be a long night, I can tell.

We walk silently up the stairs, as if the silence will extend our poor endurance of physical activity. It seems like forever. I can feel my heart in my throat, my lungs begging for more oxygen, and my legs burning. But it is exhilarating and breathtaking, the euphoria of being ostensibly stress free and given time to wallow in my thoughts without interruption. I'm enjoying the simple act of walking up the stairs way too much. The younger version of my father would've liked this. He would've acted like a romantic even though he hates the seemingly unequal aspect of romance. He would always say that guys having to buy the chocolate and flowers was unfair, especially considering that he had been a very broke adult with first-world issues.

"I, for one, love chocolate a lot more than your mother does, thank you very much, and I have bills to pay," he said to me once before Valentine's Day when I was nine. Though he said this, he would've planned days in advance for a candlelight dinner for two on top of the Tower: just the two of them.

Would have.

I have not seen that side of my father in months.

The view from the top of the Tower of Rookwood High School is not beautiful, but it is insightful. It shows me cars on the street, the miniature people and the beauty that comes from being at bird's-eye view. The streetlights have turned on, and they give a yellowish glow to the dull asphalt. There is a teacher who is walking toward her car, a gargantuan cart trailing behind her. Although I have never met her, I notice how her shoulders sag, and her posture is less than perfect. Her jacket, even from here, looks askew. Everything is so . . . small. It shows me how frail and fragile my surroundings are. I see the temporariness of my existence. It opens my eyes to an entirely new and foreign world, one run by emotion and passion, not by grade point average or the third question on my last Calculus test. Actually, maybe that does matter. I think I got that wrong. But anyway, that's not what my ever-intelligent point was supposed to be. What was going to be the most philosophical, metaphysical, and abstract internal monologue of my life is ruined when something hits my face. And there it is again, the flowery spawn of Satan.

"That's yours." Adelaide smirks, something that I have come to enjoy instead of despise. I grab the blanket from where it has fallen at my feet. After I do that, I wrap the fabric around my shoulders like a cape and bow deeply.

"Thank you, m'lady, for the honor of wearing a cape that has been blessed by the throne of hell itself."

Adelaide and Zaidan laugh. "The pleasure is all mine, good sir!" Adelaide responds.

"Oh, and me too"—Zaidan bats his eyelashes—"*good sir.*"

"If you keep talking like that, your bruise is going to get worse."

Zaidan is confused, and so am I. "What bru—*ow*! What the hell!"

Adelaide has given Zaidan an audible, solid punch on the arm and she steps back, satisfied. "*That* bruise," she says.

Zaidan laughs despite being in pain. He lugs a sleeping bag to one side of the area. "All right," he gestures to the entire floor. "Spread out, younglings. I don't want to see any PDA."

"What the hell, Zaidan?" I say, impervious to his comments anymore. Nevertheless, we have set up our bags a couple of feet apart.

We slide into our sleeping bags, our breaths clearly visible, curling like smoke and disappearing along with our worries. The feeling is like electricity, the invisible sparks of happiness emitting from our fingers and returning with a satisfying crackling noise. I have never felt more alive in my life. The exhilarating satisfaction of lying there, doing absolutely nothing, means the world to me. It makes me feel whole, for just a moment, the happiness clouding our eyes with satisfaction. I enjoy this, I really do.

Laughter bubbles in my chest, and I have the need to laugh, relieved that, for at least one time in my tragically dull life, I can do this. And so I laugh.

Moments later, I feel a hand lightly placed on my arm. "You okay?" Adelaide's eyes are wide with concern.

"Yeah, I'm okay. It's just, after years of feeling like a caged bird, I feel a bit free." I smile at her knowingly, hoping she'll understand the reference I'm making to the beginning of the school year, the first time we met.

She smiles back at me.

"Same, for some reason, I feel like 'the menace of the years find and shall find me unafraid.'"

I chuckle. "Is 'Invictus' your life motto? You know, just the whole 'screw it' mentality?"

"Why not?" She shrugs, pulling a strand of renegade hair behind one of her ears. "Is your life goal to be Maya Angelou?"

"Yes, I want to be a completely unprecedented, ingenious African American woman when I grow up."

She giggles, simultaneously shaking her head. "That's better than most people's ambitions in life."

"Ambitions," I say.

"Yeah," she says, shivering.

"Here, just bring your—you know—sleeping bag," I say, gesturing to her sleeping bag.

"Eloquent," she remarks, raising her eyebrows, but she does anyway. In a few moments, she's tucked under a mass of navy-blue fabric, looking up at the stars with me.

"Ambitions," she says.

"Ambitions," I repeat.

"Why do people say 'dreams' instead of ambitions?" she wonders aloud.

"I know," I empathize. "Once I had a dream that I was stuck in a toaster."

She laughs. "Please fulfill that dream." She reaches out and pinches my arm hard.

"Besides, you're too pale."

"Better than being burnt to a crisp. Literally," I retort. "I'd rather have my epidermis, thank you very much."

She lets out an airy laugh. "Who needs an epidermis anyway? Completely useless." For a few moments, all we hear is the wind, filling in the gaps of our conversation. "But anyway, what are your dreams—sorry, *ambitions*? What do you want to do?"

"To be honest?" I say. "No fucking clue."

"To be honest?" she repeats. "That's the answer I was expecting."

"Good," I say. "Because that's the only answer you're going to get for a while."

"Perfectly fine with me."

A part of me shakes my head in despair, disappointed that I have almost given up on myself. The other stands arrogantly, arms folded, refusing to give up. *Life goes on*, it says, *and so will we*. The most horrible, eye-opening realization is that I don't know how I feel, and that is one of the only things that truly scares me.

I suddenly realize I've almost forgotten about Zaidan. I turn to see him on his phone, a sad smile on his face. I decide that he needs to be left alone, swirling in his own world for now. There is no need for me to interrupt.

Adelaide and I talk some more, discussing *Animal Farm*, which we both read in middle school. It was nice to talk about something that I enjoyed learning about.

"But I don't understand!" Her voice is animated and approximately two octaves higher. It's always like this when she talks about something she's passionate about. "If the dogs were that vulnerable, going off of when Boxer had one of them under his hoof, then why didn't Napoleon use Boxer as protection? He was gullible anyway, as Orwell himself described. And what was the point of killing Boxer? He was on Napoleon's side! It just doesn't make any sense!"

She looks at me for an adequate response. Her brown eyes are wild and fierce, as if daring me to challenge her. I won't.

"You're completely right," I say, trying to keep from smiling amusedly and giving away that I have not been paying attention at all.

"Of course I am!" she says matter-of-factly.

Conversation slows from there, as if someone has turned off a tap in our heads, forcing us to stop. So instead, I look at Zaidan. He has not said a word after my talk with Adelaide. He huddles under his sleeping bag, his phone's brightness covering his face with a thin layer of white light. The color matches his fingers, which are gripping the corners of the phone tightly. "Zaidan?" I say. He does a jump of sorts, remembering where he is. "You okay?"

"Yeah," he says apprehensively. "I just . . . oh fuck it." He stands up. "I need to go, okay?"

The look on his face is so desperate that I concede without asking why.

"Good," he says. "I'll pick you up in the morning."

"Tell her I said hello," Adelaide says without skipping a beat.

"Bye," I say dryly.

It's just me and Adelaide left on the Tower.

"Is silence our adversary again?" I ask.

She shakes her head. "No. Not this time," she says.

"Okay," I say tentatively. "How do you think Ara is?"

And then it happens, the inevitable moment. The first time that I ever see Adelaide Lillvik-Trumbull cry. A weight drops in my stomach, pulling me down. Somehow, I can't move. Wait, no, let's cut the bullshit; I *can* move. It's just that if I do, I have no idea what the hell I'm going to do. The one thing that comes up is my mother's signature awkward-shoulder-pat-and-silence move. But that's not an option. I get up, my hands twitching uncomfortably. The painful truth of emotion is that not all of it is good.

I reach Adelaide. She wipes her tears, rubbing her skin so hard that it stretches and reddens. I empathize. I hate people seeing me cry. But if Adelaide doesn't cease crying, I think I might start. Already, I have started blinking my eyes furiously. I hate it when I cry, but I hate it more when I see other people cry and I can't do anything about it.

Oh, *fuck it*.

I stand there, an arm's length away, patting her on the back. She looks at me amusedly, even in her sudden state of dysphoria.

"Your tact, or lack thereof, is frankly invigorating," she says.

She gets up and puts her hands on the ledge. She hoists herself up and sits quietly on the ledge, her legs dangling dangerously over the edge. She taps the area next to her, gesturing for me to sit.

"You'd think there would be stars out," she says. "It was supposed to be a glorious night. But there are no stars."

"Are stars necessary to have a glorious night?" I ask.

"No," she says thoughtfully. "Clouds can be beautiful too." She looks up. "See? The gigantic mass of evaporated H_2O."

"Is that scientifically correct?" I inquire.

She shrugs her shoulders. "No fucking clue."

I look at her in disbelief. "You *didn't*."

"What?" she says blankly.

"You—*you just cursed*."

"Oh shit," she mutters. Then, her eyes widen. She looks out, leaning her head up toward the starless sky, and takes a deep breath. "I've got to admit, it feels nice to do that after such a long time."

"Why don't you curse?"

She sighs heavily. "I've never really told anyone about this . . ." she trails off.

"You don't have to tell me," I assure her.

"No," she says. "I should tell you." She takes a deep breath.

"When I was fourteen, I had a huge fight with my mom." She chuckles. "Now that I think about it properly, I can't even remember what it was about . . . Anyway, let's just say I said some horrible things to her . . ." I nod, encouraging her to go on. "That included some cursing, and I told myself that I'd never curse in front of her. After that, it just sort of escalated, and I ended up not cursing at all."

"Am I encouraging you to curse?" I say worriedly. "Am I being a bad influence?"

Adelaide laughs. "Troye, you're absolutely fine. It's just me."

She stays silent and raises one of her hands, ruffling her own hair, and one of her sleeves falls. Then, I see red. Literally.

"What the hell is that?" I grab one of her arms.

I see straight crimson lines near her wrists. I take a closer look.

"Thank God." I can breathe again, relieved that Adelaide's wrists are intact.

I look at her face. "Why do you have red marker on your arms?"

"Let's just say this . . ." She looks uncomfortable. "A . . . a friend of mine, she cuts. And I draw these"—she pokes one of the lines with her nail—"to remind her of the impact she's making on people around her, not just herself."

"It's Ara, isn't it?"

She looks down.

"Does Zaidan know?"

She shakes her head. "It's the same concept that Zaidan told us in the car: she doesn't want him to see her like this. Besides," she says. "I don't think it's my place to tell him."

"Bullshit."

"What?" She looks at me, her eyes wide with shock.

"I said, 'bullshit.' Nobody can say that and still be justified. Adelaide, one day she could decide that she wants to—to *kill herself*. We can't let that happen."

There is a charged silence before I add to my monologue. "And maybe the only reason she's still cutting is because Zaidan doesn't know. We're preventing him from knowing and essentially putting Ara in more harm."

She shakes her head. "What the hell was I thinking?" She swings her legs back around the ledge, facing our now-cold sleeping bags.

"Should we go find where Zaidan went?" I suggest.

"No," she says, wringing her hands. The cracking of her knuckles is slightly eerie in the dark environment. "I already know where he is."

Zaidan

THE FIRST TIME I KNOW SOMETHING IS WRONG IS WHEN I GET the text. It's from Ara. I eagerly open up the message.

Hey Del! I see that you took the razors under the sink and in the cabinet. Thanks for that. I don't know what I would do if I still had them.

A couple of seconds later, like clockwork, she has added eloquently:

Don't yell at Adelaide. She was just trying to help.

I grip the sides of my phone. I have to go. I look at Adelaide and Troye. They're talking quietly, and I decide not to disturb them, but I need to go. Troye, right on cue, startles me out of my stupor.

"Zaidan? You okay?"

"Yeah," I say, fighting to keep emotion out of my voice. "I just . . . oh fuck it." I stand up, the sleeping bag falling to my feet. "I need to go, okay?"

Troye nods, looking pretty confused.

"Good," I say. "I'll pick you up in the morning."

"Tell her I said hello," Adelaide speaks suddenly, in a monotonous voice.

"Bye," Troye says, visibly crestfallen.

I would apologize, but I can't.

I climb down the steps and sprint past the gym and out the front doors.

I push the key into ignition and the car starts without its usual groans and squeals of the engine. Pulling out of the parking lot, I grip the steering wheel with both hands and look straight ahead. *I will get there, I will get there,* I chant in my head, as if the mantra is the only thing that will help me get to Ara.

I drive for the next ten minutes. My heart is pounding in my chest and I feel a sudden sense of emptiness. This emptiness, ironically, consumes me. I feel apathy, an emotion I have never felt before. It scares me. The act of feeling nothing is an emotion that is entirely new to me. But for now, I must deal with it. It feels like an indicator of the oncoming storm. I don't know what I will say. It has been seven years since I met Ara and for the first time, I have nothing to say to her.

I pull up at her house. The lights are on but nevertheless an aura of gloominess radiates from the lit windows. An unsettling anxiety pools in the bottom of my stomach. I walk briskly to the front door. I hesitate before ringing the doorbell—I hear music. I strain my ears and hear Logan at his piano. I'm not sure what he's playing, but it sounds good.

Logan opens the door just as I am about to ring again. He looks up at me, his bespectacled eyes evidently confused.

"Zaidan? What're you doing here?"

"Hi," I say, forcing a smile on my face, scratching the back of my neck with one hand nervously. "I'm here to see Ara."

"Um . . ." He looks backward. "Give me a second."

He sprints toward the dining room where I presume his mom is working. I hear murmurs and then loud, clumsy, and fast footsteps toward me. "My mom says you can come in," Logan says, breathing loudly. He may be a musical prodigy, but he has been cursed with a lanky and sickly physique, and, along with it, exercise-induced asthma. He pulls out a bright-red inhaler and in seconds his breathing stops sounding like Darth Vader's.

"Thanks," I say. "What were you playing?"

He beams. The only thing that he shows true passion about is playing the piano. The thing I love about this boy is that no one forced him to play piano. In fact, when he was in third grade, he told his mom that he was joining an afterschool extracurricular which was all five days of the school week. She was apprehensive, but she agreed. Day after day he came home late, looking a bit tired, but with a smile on his face.

One day, Logan asked Ara if they could switch beds. Ara had a twin-sized bed, but Logan had a queen. Ara was confused, but she said yes anyway. A couple of months passed and one day Ara heard music coming from his room. She opened the door and found a grand piano sitting in the middle of his room, his new twin bed barely fitting between the wall and the beautiful instrument. Sitting on a dusty piano bench was none other than Logan himself, playing away. It turns out that instead of attending the club he said he would, he walked down to one of the restaurants five minutes from his school and volunteered to play the piano for customers. His audience loved it so much that they gave him money.

Every day he saved and made a little more. He used that money to buy a secondhand piano. It was antiquated, but usable. Assuring the owners that his parents had agreed, he lugged up the piano to his room with their help. Since then, he had never stopped playing.

"I was playing 'Boléro, Opus 19' by Chopin."

"That sounded beautiful." I smile.

"Thank you!" He usually doesn't take compliments well, believing his music to be inherently flawed. "Well, I'd better get *Bach* to it." He giggles maniacally.

I shake my head, chuckling. "I get it. Nice pun." But he has already dashed up the stairs in record time. I hear him play with more vigor now, determined to live up to the compliment he just received.

I follow the same path he has taken upstairs. However, instead of running to an awaiting piano, I walk slowly to Ara's room, the first one on the right. I turn the doorknob gently and for the first time, Ara is in a sitting position, one hand clutching her phone and the other holding on to what seems to be a mug of hot chocolate.

"I knew you'd show up." Her voice is dry and crackly, wisps of her dialogue lost in the air between us. "I knew it."

"You know me too well, I guess," I whisper, not even sure if she heard me.

She puts down her phone and the mug and burrows into her bed, letting the quilt cover her entire body. I can only see her closed eyes. They are shut tight, like she's trying to block out her painful existence. The silence is there, but we hardly notice it. It remains the elephant in the room.

"You know . . ." I say, my voice surprisingly firm. "My family history is riddled with Alzheimer's."

She doesn't respond, but I have anticipated that. I continue anyway.

"And you know, one day I'm probably going to have it because of that damned mutated gene."

No response, but that's okay.

"You know, my grandfather died recently. He had Alzheimer's and cancer." I gulp, trying to gather the courage to say this (and to get rid of the lump in my throat). There is no indication that she's listening to me. "When he woke up one day, he couldn't remember my mom or any of his other kids. My mom, she was heartbroken, and that made me feel like shit. I didn't know my grandfather that much. It had absolutely no effect on me when he died. But my mom was sobbing. She didn't go to work for two weeks and it took her two days to finally eat something. That made me feel like the most heartless little shit in the entire world."

She doesn't say anything, but her eyelashes are lining with tears. But I continue. I must. "But you know what the worst thing was?"

Her eyes, still mostly closed, are streaming with tears.

"That day, when he had woken up, he asked for my grandmother. He had forgotten that she died two years before in her sleep. He had to relive the grief of her death. When asked about it, he said he felt a little better than he should because he found out it was in her sleep. He said it eased the pain because she had gone naturally."

I reach into the blanket and find her hand and grip it tight. "If I have learned one damn thing from this event, it's that I don't want to do that. I don't want to wake up one morning and not know that the strangers surrounding my bed are actually my kids. And when I wake up, I don't want to say 'Where's Arabella?' and have everyone look at each other and shake their heads. I don't want to relive the death of the girl I love, who everyone else knows as the girl who committed suicide."

Her grip on my hand is almost hurting me. She opens her eyes, sits up, and wraps her arms around me. We sit like that for a long time, arms enveloping the other, using each other for support. My shoulder is wet.

"Um . . . guys?" We pull apart as Logan stands at the door, a piece of sheet music in his hands. "I think I finally got this right. Do you mind if you take a minute to hear it?"

I am about to answer when Ara speaks first. "Yeah, sure," she says. She pushes the covers off her body.

"What're those?" Logan says, pointing to the bandages on her arms.

She smiles sadly. "It's nothing," she says cheerily. "Let's hear this piece, shall we?"

Logan looks like he wants to say something, but then he turns around and gestures us out of the hall and into his room.

It's the same as the last time I saw it, the piano in the center of the room, taking up most of the space. It's been used so much that looking at it from a distance, one would think it was in disrepair. It was antediluvian, the wood chipped and the ivory keys fragmented.

"Felix is getting old," I remark. Logan had named his piano Felix, partially because he thought the name was cool and partially because it meant "lucky" in Latin.

"Yeah, he is," Logan says sadly. He sits on the jet-black piano bench, fragments of its faux leather coming apart. He puts his hands delicately on the keys. And he plays.

He finishes three resounding notes, and then starts play faster than I can physically comprehend. Then the song slows, his beautiful legato notes that grace the air around him. He plays for what seems like an eternity, but I don't mind. When the final notes die down, I snap back into reality. Logan looks at us with expectant eyes.

"Did you like it?"

"That was amazing," Ara says. She walks over, sits down next to him, and gives him a hug. I look away, as if watching their rare show of affection is intruding on their privacy. So instead, I turn my attention to something that catches my eye. A single poster filling a small space on the whitewashed walls: Juilliard School of Music. It is fairly new, I can tell, because it still has a shiny gleam that all new posters have, still intact, all the edges lacking a single nick.

"Yeah, I know," Logan says, sighing. "I'll never get in."

I turn to him. "You kidding?" I put my hand on his shoulder. "I think they'll be begging for you as soon as you get out of high school."

He grins, the fire in his eyes brighter than ever. "You think so?"

And of course, I make the stereotypical decision of saying, "I know so." But it is worth it, seeing the happiness on his face.

"It's time for us to go now." Ara pulls on my arm. Her eyes are melancholy but beautiful. They remind me of everything I love: the sea, the sky, the bluest blue in the world. Then it hits me: I love her, too. I really do.

We sit on her bed, the quilt now pushed to the side, seemingly forgotten. "So what were you saying?" Her voice is hollow and she looks down.

"Yeah . . . sorry; that was overly dramatic."

"No." Her head snaps up. "It wasn't." Her eyes lower to the ground. "I especially appreciate the part where you told me about that random girl you loved."

I feel heat rising into my cheeks. "Can you tell her I wasn't lying?"

"I don't know if I'm right," she says, leaning closer, "but I think this girl, Ara—Ana—whatever her name is—I think she feels the same way about you. But I'm not really sure. She kind of doesn't believe in love."

I, for some reason, feel confident. I smirk and say, "Well, it's been seven years since we met. I'm not surprised she finds me attractive."

She mirrors my expression and says fiercely, "If she didn't, I don't think she would be dating you. I think *you're* the lucky one in your relationship with her."

I grin. "I agree."

Before we can continue our banter the doorbell rings. I hear the grand piano down the hall stop producing notes, and loud footfalls trodding down the stairs.

"Hi, are Ara and Zaidan here?" The unmistakable voice of none other than Adelaide Lillvik-Trumbull graces my ears.

"Yeah, they're upstairs." I hear Logan running back up the stairs. Then I hear two pairs of hesitant steps coming up.

"You okay?" I say to Ara. She nods. Approximately two seconds later, someone knocks on the door. I call to them. "Come in!"

"Hi," Troye says. "Are we intruding?"

I smile. "Not at all. Come sit." I wave them over and they oblige hesitantly, Adelaide sitting comfortably cross-legged.

"So . . . how're you doing?" Adelaide, for the first time ever, sounds quiet.

"Exceedingly okay," Ara says. "Just needed some"—she looks at Zaidan—"motivation."

"That's good," Troye says without a hint of adroitness. He pats Ara's shoulder a couple of times. "Good to know you're feeling better."

"Thanks."

There is an expected moment of uncomfortable silence in which all participants (including myself) look at the others with crippling inelegance.

"Guys," Adelaide unfolds her legs. "Let's go for a walk."

"I'm cool with it." Troye stands up, putting on a jacket. "Just around the neighborhood." He looks at Ara and me. "It'll be fun."

I shrug. "That's fine with me." I look at Arabella, giving her hand a small squeeze. I can't tell what she's saying; her face is pallid and unreadable. However, I know my eyes are saying *please* repeatedly.

She gives in. "Oh, all right."

"Get out," she says promptly. The three of us are slightly offended.

"What for?" I say.

"I need to change." I survey her clothes, a Maiden Voyage T-shirt and black pajama pants.

"No, you don't," I say. "You look wonderful."

She rolls her eyes. "You're just saying that because you're, well, you."

"If you don't leave this room right now, I can assure you I have other means of persuasion," I tease.

She crosses her arms defiantly. "No."

I smirk. "Then you leave me no choice." I wrap my hands around her abdomen and lift her up. Ignoring her complaints, I run outside her room. Even though I am shorter than her, she's not that hard to carry.

When we have reached the front door, I say, "Grab her shoes!"

"Got them," Adelaide says promptly.

After running for a couple more seconds, I stop and set her down on the hood of my car.

"Look! That wasn't that bad!"

Adelaide catches up in a few moments and cheekily hands Ara her shoes, tattered white Vans that have faded to a lowly gray. "Here you go Ara; you forgot these on the way out."

"Of course," Ara says sarcastically, tucking a strand of hair behind her ear. "I must've forgotten them while walking out."

Adelaide blinks, hesitating for a moment then smiling tentatively. "You must've. Good thing I got them out of the house."

Ara mumbles almost indistinguishable words under her breath while shoving on her shoes. "If anyone from Rookwood sees me like this, I'm dead, and before I die, I swear I will send you three to hell first."

"We'll be honored," Troye says, managing to hear what she muttered. "I need to talk to Satan about getting my throne back."

Adelaide and Ara laugh ridiculously loud.

"You?" Adelaide incredulously. "If anyone out of the four of us, it would be Zaidan who would be the queen of hell."

I do a double take. "Excuse me? The *queen?*"

Ara smiles with a faux sympathy. "Title assignments are based on the measured levels of dramatic tendencies." Her voice is like a stereotypical white girl's. She leans closer to Zaidan, still sitting on the top of his car. "And you, ma'am, are a queen at the far right of the drama spectrum."

Zaidan looks offended for a moment; then he shrugs his shoulders and nods. "Yeah, you're probably right."

Ara giggles. "I knew it."

I pat my car, suddenly inspired. "Let's go back to the Tower," I say.

Troye shrugs. "Fine with me." Adelaide has a similar reaction.

I look at Ara, begging with my eyes yet again. "All right, fine," she says. "But I need to go get my sleeping bag."

"There's no need." I smirk. "You can share mine."

She mirrors my expression. "Okay. Let's go."

The ride back to school is loud and boisterous. I prefer it a lot more this way, rather than being enveloped by silence. Ara seems to be regenerated, a happier version of herself. Isn't that interesting? I've just thought of something. Every person has different sides, right? What if all their lives, someone has known a person, but just one side of them? What happens when they find out about the other sides? They have suddenly met an entirely new person. What can they do but to adapt to the person they have just encountered?

This is why I want to know every single aspect of Ara. Every single side. That way, there will be no surprises in our future.

As we pull up to the school again, I can see the basketball team walking out, Di Masi giving them stiff nods of approval. I turn off the headlights and lead the car straight to the parking spot we were in earlier. We sit still, not moving a muscle until Di Masi's car has driven past the corner and out of sight.

"All right then!" I say, practically leaping out of the car.

"A bit excited, aren't you?" Ara says.

"An entire night with my best friends and girlfriend in a freezing cold environment that can't even make it up by having *stars*?" I grin. "This is going to be awesome."

"Freezing cold, you say?" Ara says worriedly. She gestures to her clothes again. I notice her arms have been layered with goose bumps. She rubs her arms, trying to get warmth to appear. I open the trunk and hand her a black jacket of mine. It doesn't fit her, but she slips it on anyway, the sleeves covering her hands.

"Thanks," she states. "Let's go then, shall we?"

I bow deeply, my nose almost touching my knees. "Your wish is my command."

"Get up, young knight," Ara says. "You are permitted to rise."

I stand up to my full height, which, awkwardly enough, doesn't match Ara's height.

"Trying to look intimidating?" Ara smiles, tiptoeing so she can look down at me.

"Is it working?" I ask. When she shakes her head, I stick my tongue out at her.

We enter the school, and this time we don't have to hide. Climbing up the stairs, we slow down and make our breathing shallow because we can hear a voice.

"—I know, I know, Aaliyah. I understand. I'll try to be there. No, I can't guarantee it."

There is a long pause. "Fine. Okay." Another pause. "I love you too. Bye."

Xavier, with his posture poor, is sitting on the ledge of the opening on our right. He has a melancholy aura about him, something that's strangely comforting. It's upsetting to think about; comfort shouldn't be obtained like that. It feels *wrong*, like stealing a prized possession from an old lady. I feel like a bully, one who puts others down just to make myself feel better.

Xavier sighs. Although it is a fairly windy night he is wearing a T-shirt, and goose bumps line his arms.

Adelaide coughs intentionally. This is a bad move—Xavier jumps like he's been facing the barrel of a shotgun and nearly falls off the Tower. He looks at us for a second, and then says, "Hold on a minute." He looks over the edge down onto the balcony below. "Yep." He chuckles, running a hand through his hair. "I kicked my glasses down there."

"Oh," Adelaide replies. "Sorry?"

Xavier smiles. "It's okay." He pulls out another pair from his pocket. "I always keep an extra with me, for some reason."

"Perhaps because it's written in the code of the universe that one day, some random kid would scare you, and that you would kick your glasses off a ledge. So, intuitively, you have an extra pair," Ara thinks out loud.

"Interesting thought, stranger, but it may be that I keep an extra pair of glasses in my pocket because I have a two-year-old niece who is fond of breaking them. Maybe it has nothing to do with the silent student that makes her presence known by coughing."

Ara laughs. "Well said." She then holds her hand out. "Arabella. Pleasure to meet you."

Xavier takes her hand. "Xavier. Likewise."

"Are you a student? I haven't seen you around," she asks inquisitively. Xavier, Troye, and Adelaide laugh simultaneously while I look on in amusement.

"No, actually," Xavier has a grin on his face. "I'm the Rookwood High School orchestra conductor."

Arabella, no matter what she's feeling right now, looks unfazed. "Oh, okay. Sorry about the misunderstanding," she states calmly.

There is a moment of awkward silence; then, Xavier says inelegantly, "Well, I'd better go and get my glasses." He looks at Troye and Adelaide. "I'll see you two in class on Monday." He walks over to the stone steps leading back to the blessed heaters of the school.

It's okay, I decide, that I don't feel warmth. I can feel my heart beating out of my chest, signaling my successful survival, and that is enough. The cold air is soothing, even though it's harsh against my skin, forming goose bumps. It reminds me that I'm merely human, susceptible to the veritable harms of the world. This is an important lesson: we are not impermeable. In fact, I'd say we're one of the most vulnerable creatures on the Earth. Our main downfall is ourselves.

Taking a gulp of air and feeling the stinging sensation in my lungs is a marvelous experience. Depending on oxygen can frustrate the vainest of egos, but it should be our strength, not something to be ashamed of.

Weakness is strength; nothing to be ashamed of.

"Hey." Ara's voice is slightly disconcerting because she sounds unsure. I hate when she does that; I feel like this voice of doubt is my fault. For this reason, I attempt to smile.

"I'm fine," I say, knowing what she wants to know.

"Fine as in actually fine, or fine as in not-fine-but-you-don't-want-to-tell-me fine?"

"Fine as in exceedingly attractive fine," I retort.

All doubts are washed away from her face as she laughs. That's much better. "I can vouch for that," she remarks.

"Guys, come over here!" Adelaide yells from the other side of the oval area.

"You're going to freeze to death over there!"

In my dazed, epiphanic trance, I have completely missed setting up the entire sleeping bag arrangements. I am slightly relieved that I didn't have to do any of the work.

I walk over and curl up into one of the warm expanses of fabric. It feels weird, though, having warmth soothe the freezing skin that I appreciated just moments before. And then I have yet another of my dramatic realizations: it is because humans are vulnerable that we have support. However, some people may not have it.

I myself enjoy the cold, but that does not make up for the fact that it could kill me. It's good that I have a warm layer of fabric covering my body. But what happens if one loves the cold and doesn't have anything to defend himself with? This could apply to so many different situations that it's frightening.

". . . and that, my friends, is why I think *1984* is the best book that depicts a dystopian society."

"I think you should be given medals for the capability to speak that much," I say honestly, cracking a joke because I have no idea what Adelaide's going on about.

"Would you like that bruised arm to start bleeding now?" Adelaide says fiercely. "Honestly, if it wasn't for *And Then There Were None*, I would say that *1984* is my favorite book."

"I love *And Then There Were None!*" Ara says excitedly, and the girls launch into a conversation about the characters in the book. Troye turns to me.

"It's funny how they get so excited about something as trivial as books."

I raise my eyebrows. "Don't let Adelaide hear you say that. You might ruin your chances."

He turns red, which is incredibly entertaining. "It's not like that," he whispers.

"Sure," I say amusedly. We drop the subject after this because I know I shouldn't push him too much.

"Zaidan! Troye!" Adelaide gestures for us to listen to her.

Adelaide

"WE'RE GOING TO PLAY THE GAME THAT ISN'T A GAME," I announce jovially. Taking in Troye and Zaidan's confused looks, I clarify. "The game that Pomeroy made us play ages ago." They still look confused. Oh, the poor, imbecilic children. "You know? The catalyst of our friendship? The game eloquently called 'Tell Me Your Favorite Color and Your Deepest, Darkest Secrets.' I'm sure you remember it."

"Oh, I remember that!" Zaidan shouts.

"As do I," Troye states calmly. "But why are we playing this game that isn't a game?"

Ara furrows her eyebrows. "Because we know that Zaidan's favorite color is green and you're an only child and Adelaide likes books and I like tapping my feet to music. However, I don't know if Zaidan likes books or if Adelaide likes green or if you like tapping your feet to music."

She tucks her knees under her arms, close to her chest. "And I most certainly don't know, but would not object to knowing, your secrets that should probably never see the light of day."

Troye shrugs. "I'm in, just because you managed to remember all of that."

"Why not?" Zaidan concedes.

"I'll go first," I say. I lean closer to the others. "When I first met you two," I gesture to Zaidan and Arabella, "I thought your name was Zeke." Ara bursts out laughing, while Zaidan crosses his arms and pouts.

Taking one look at Zaidan, Ara laughs hysterically. "What—did—we—tell—you," she manages to say between laughter and gasps of air, "*queen.*"

Upon hearing this, Zaidan pouts even more. Then he alleviates all thoughts of seriousness by cracking a smile. Ah, there's the Zaidan I know.

"Ara, you go," Zaidan says animatedly. Ara obliges.

"My . . . favorite band is . . ." She points to her T-shirt. "The Maiden Voyage."

Zaidan rolls his eyes. "We all know that. Tell us something else. Preferably about your Apollo-esque hot boyfriend."

"All right, all right," she says, grinning. "So this 'hot boyfriend' of mine," she looks at Zaidan and winks. "I think he's great and all"—she throws us a sorrowful look—"but I think he's in love with his car." She flutters her eyelids pathetically, and before Zaidan can protest, she speaks again.

"I mean, Del, you should see the way he looks at it. You should too—was it Thomas? Tyler? Oh no, it's Troye, right?" She blinks lazily, throwing a wink at Zaidan. "I'd never thought that I would have anything against hybrid cars, but this one just irks me. You know, I just want Zaidan to like me."

Before she can go on, however, Zaidan finally gets a chance to defend his honor. "I'm thoroughly infatuated with my lady, thank you." He snakes a hand around her waist.

Troye smiles sweetly, his pearly white teeth shining in the moonlight.

Ara chuckles. "Troye, it's your turn."

Troye sighs. The smile on his face is gone. I don't like that, not at all. "All right, so this is something I didn't tell you when we were all over at Zaidan's." He sighs, his shoulders are slumped, and even though his long legs aren't folded, he looks like he is partially cowering. "I know why my parents moved to Georgia. And no, it wasn't because of the arrest."

We all wait patiently, not daring to say a word. "A couple of months before, well, my dad's 'problem' got really serious, I heard a phone conversation between my dad and, well, all that I know is that her name is Lavinia, and she's *'enchanting in bed'* and he *'can't wait until my mom leaves for another conference.'*"

We don't process the meaning of his words until after a couple of seconds.

Ara's reaction is to clap her hands to her mouth, and Zaidan tightens his grip on her waist, gazing at the floor with a solemn expression. I don't know what I should do.

"Well, obviously, I told him that I heard his little conversation. I gave him an ultimatum: 'you tell her or I will.' Let's just say that dinner was cut short that night. It wasn't a whole soap opera thing where the *affair*"—he spits the word out like it's poison—"lasts for years and my dad bribes me with, like, three hundred dollars in cash every week. My mom was about to sign divorce papers. It was going to be really messy, I could tell, because my mom and dad worked together."

Troye's knuckles are white; he is gripping his sleeping bag far too tight. There will be nail marks in the center of his palm.

"But she *forgave him*. We have a happy, perfect family again, right? But I can't do it. I can't bring myself to consider him as a father again. You should've heard the way he was talking to *the beautiful Lavinia*." His voice is icy. "Whenever he's affectionate to my mom in front of me—ugh, I just want to smack him. I mean, not that it happens very often these days."

By now, I have realized that I must react to this in some way. So, I do the same thing my mother does to me when I'm unhappy.

I slip my hand in his and rub soothing circles on the back of his hand with my thumb. I can almost hear my mother's comforting voice, murmuring indistinct words to me. "Is there anything we can do to help you feel better?"

"No, honestly, it's fine," he says. This is how Troye is. He may seem like a very uncomfortably comfortable, plaid-donning, nonchalant person, but he takes his feelings out of his own hands, puts them on a dusty shelf, and supports other people.

"Look at that," Ara says, probably trying to diffuse the fog-like tension. "Stars."

We separate into our own groups, Zaidan and Ara on the other side of the Tower and Troye and I sitting on the ledge where we were mere hours ago. Our hands are intertwined, but not in a sappy, romantic way. He needs support and I am there to provide it.

I dangle my legs over the edge, my heels gently tapping the stone exterior walls of the building.

"Stop that," Troye says, his voice quiet.

"What?" I say.

"The tapping. You're going to accidentally fall over the edge or something. I think the three of us would not like that." He looks over his shoulder at Arabella and Zaidan, who are sharing a sleeping bag, Zaidan's arm around her shoulder. It's almost comical, considering her legs reach farther than his. They are both sound asleep.

"Déjà vu, no?" I remark.

"How so?" he says dryly.

"Zaidan and Ara are asleep and you and I are looking at the sky."

"Oh," he says. "I thought you meant about you not dying."

"No, but I do appreciate that you would not like it if I died."

"I wouldn't like it if anyone died."

"Anyone? Even someone particularly horrible?"

"Rights are for the ones that people don't want to give rights to."

I stare at him for about a minute. "Brilliant."

He makes a facial gesture that vaguely looks like a smile, but not quite. "Thank you."

"No problem," I say, knowing that I am disrupting the careful balance of silence.

"Shit, Troye! Adelaide! Get off the damn ledge!"

My eyes snap open.

"Whasthematter?" I hear Troye say sleepily.

"You guys slept on the damn ledge! You could've died! You could've been seen!"

I smile, rubbing the sleep out of my eyes. "Nice Harry Potter reference Ara, although I doubt that Molly Weasley would ever curse in front of her children outside of wartime."

"Dammit," Ara says.

They act extremely normal, as if nothing major happened last night. They are very good at it: avoiding issues. I wish I was better at it.

"But really, we're surprised that you didn't fall off the ledge; we thought you would've broken a bone or two by now."

"Sorry to disappoint you," Troye mutters, standing up straight and stretching, his fingertips almost touching the stone ceiling.

"It's okay," Zaidan says cheekily. "Try harder next time."

"Will do," I say.

Silently and almost automatically, we all start packing up our things.

Troye

WE HEAD TO BARAKAH'S, WHERE ADELAIDE PICKS UP HER CAR. She offers to drop me home, which makes sense since we live close together (despite this, I've never been to her house).

We exchange simple but meaningful goodbyes, and I head into my house, already prepared for an intervention.

"Troye James Saavedra! Where have you been? Your mother and I have been so worried about you! This was a completely irresponsible thing to do."

"I left a note on the table," I mumble. "I told you I was going to Ara's."

"Just—just sit down." We walk into the dining room where my mother is waiting, her lips pursed.

"Troye, sit down."

"Yes," I say under my breath. "I heard."

"Excuse me?" My father's voice is agitated. I savor it.

"Nothing," I whisper.

"Where were you?" Unsurprisingly, my mother's voice is cold.

"At Ara's."

There is complete silence.

I look at my mother rather than staring down my crimson-faced dad. Her shoulders sag, and her eyes are dim. She has sable circles under her eyes.

"Mom," I say tentatively, as she types away on her keyboard. "You should get some sleep."

And there it is: the moment this emotionally distant, stressed, and (publicly) level-headed woman snaps.

"Get some sleep? Get some *sleep*? Are you *fucking kidding me, Troye*?" She grabs the screen of her laptop and shuts it. Hard.

Then she does something completely unexpected. She grabs her laptop, picks it up, and throws it at the wall. "I'm sick of it! I've been working to keep this family afloat, ever since your dad became a drunkard, lost his job in Florida, and moved us to this goddamn town. And guess what? *He hasn't gotten a fucking job yet.* We're here because *I* got a new job."

There is a wild look in her eyes, and it is extremely unsettling.

"And then there's your friend *Ara*," she says in a condescending tone. "*Suicidal*, huh? Please. She needs to get over herself. Depression is just in your head! It's a mental thing. If she just *tries* to be a bit happier, she can get over this."

"Mom, I don't think you understand what the value of a human life is." My voice is so cold that it rivals hers. "Arabella is a wonderful person and she possesses so many qualities that you can't even comprehend." My voice rises. "And maybe you can't comprehend the value of human life because you're too busy wasting your life away doing useless shit and staying married to a loser who still pines for one more 'one-night stand' with *the elusive and beautiful Lavinia*, according to last week's phone call."

My mom looks heartbroken, much like the night that my dad told her about his affair the first time.

"Troye, go to your room." Her voice is fragile. I decide to comply.

I don't know what exactly they are talking about, but I can hear dull thuds, which indicates that someone (presumably my mother) is throwing something (presumably one of the useless trinkets in the china cabinet) at the wall. It is with this sound and the yelling that I fall asleep.

The morning air is crisp. I have always noticed that the cold is not only a feeling, like most people presume. The cold has a sharp smell.

After a while, I come to understand what unfolded downstairs last night. My mother took one single hour to tell me everything that had happened; she said she owed me that at least. It's been silent in the house since, though.

My dad and my mom, surprise, surprise, are most likely going to divorce. My mom has given him an ultimatum this time. She'll let him stay for a couple of weeks until he can find a job, and then it's goodbye. I doubt he'll try to gain custody of me because, well, there's no point. There's no way that he would win a case against my employed, less abrasive mother, and I turn eighteen soon anyway.

I'm glad that my mother finally realized that she's better off without my dad. However, both of them have stopped speaking to me. They've given me the silent treatment before, when something I have done is not up to their standards. I have a feeling that this silence is going to last much longer than any previous time. It is, in fact, an adversary, a veritable rift between me and my mother.

I appreciate January a lot more than the other winter months, partially because my birthday is in January. January twenty-sixth, to be precise. Today is January twenty-sixth. My dad has been out of the house for two weeks, and it's a relief.

My mom, being rid of that scum, looks much happier. She still won't talk to me unless it is absolutely crucial, but we have formed a silent truce, a quiet reconciliation. After all my father put her through, this is understandable. She needs to have some space after finally being set free of a marriage in shambles.

I walk in silence, the darkness of dusk surrounding me. I am alarmed by a sudden vibration coming from my pocket. I stop in my tracks to check it.

I see you outside my house; come in!

I turn to Adelaide's house. I can see her through a window. She waves awkwardly. I wave back. She gestures for me to come into the house and I oblige. I walk up the driveway and am about to ring the doorbell when she opens the door.

"Hi," she says, almost breathlessly. "Come in."

Despite having known her for a substantial amount of time and living two doors from her home, I have never been inside. It is nothing like I expected. I thought, from meeting her mother a couple of times, that her home would be a whitewashed, sophisticated, and, well, *plain* home, just like the neighborhood itself. The layout of the house is the same as mine. However, the entrance hall is a sonic blue. All the furniture has a beautiful ivory sheen.

Walking further, however, I can see that the next room is a brilliant, warm, deep red. There are tapestries depicting beautiful scenes, and kimonos hanging on the wall. Trinkets line the walls on mahogany shelves. Adelaide catches me staring in the room.

"That's Asia," she says. "We have a room in the house for every continent, except North America."

She smiles. "Europe, Asia, and Africa are on this floor while Australia and South America are downstairs in the basement. We keep a small shrine-like thing for Antarctica because we didn't bring back much from there."

"You and your mom have visited every continent?" I am impressed.

"Yeah." Her smile falters. "And my dad too."

"Oh," I say. "Sorry about that."

Her smile returns. "Anyway, I'll show you my room."

"Leave the door open!" her mother calls from the kitchen. I can tell she's smirking without even looking at her.

"Mom!" she yells back, a grin plastered on her face. "Not necessary!"

"Who knows what you teenage scoundrels could be up to when nobody's looking!"

"Thank you, Mom, for your contribution," Adelaide simpers.

"No problem."

I catch a glimpse of another room, which is a dark, bottle green. It has several shelves with ornaments and a bookshelf. I can see the Harry Potter series as well as Agatha Christie, Shakespeare, and more.

"Europe," Adelaide voices simply.

Adelaide points me to the white, wooden stairs and we climb up together. We walk down the hall, to the farthest room on the left.

She turns the doorknob, and then I hear a roar of voices, which is surprising because there are only a few people in the room. "Happy Birthday!" Ara, Zaidan, the girl from our orchestra class named Ana, and a couple of guys that I don't recognize, but I presume they are from school.

"You can vote!" One of the guys pats me on the back. "My name's Jax. There's more people coming."

"Okay," I say, not really processing what's happening. I'm just glad that this party is at Adelaide's house, to be honest. I'm not very comfortable with this many people, and I would much rather it be just the four of us. For some reason, I do a quick scan of the room and check if anyone is breaking anything or doing anything they shouldn't be doing. Zaidan is talking to Ana, and Jax has gone to talk to Adelaide. Ara is speaking animatedly to an intimidating boy with shocking purple hair, who, unsurprisingly, is wearing a Maiden Voyage hoodie. I can make out what the last pair are saying something about the album *Litost*, whatever that means.

I hear a sandy-haired boy tell a girl, "The others are coming soon."

I am alone among crowded people, so I take the time to look around Adelaide's room. The walls are a silvery gray. There are different maps of the world on her walls, and a simple wooden desk tucked into a corner of the room. There's a small, warm brown couch on the other side of the room. I decide to sit there.

While sitting, I tap my feet and look around. Then I notice something on the wall. There are names scrawled on the wall. *Jessica* is written in curlicue font, and *Jonathan* is scrawled in all caps. There is one similarity between all the names, though. They are all written in black. Then, in a bright blue, there is a note: *Write your name somewhere on the wall and/or a message if you'd like.*

I decide to take a risk and walk to her desk and grab a purple Sharpie. When I return, I start writing.

> *Hey Adelaide, for the sake of being different, I'm writing this in purple. Sorry for breaking the streak. You're a good friend.*
>
> *-Troye Saavedra (a.k.a. Washingturd)*

Then, just as I am starting to feel comfortable surrounded by strangers, I freeze. The distinct smell of whiskey is slightly overwhelming. I assumed that this wouldn't be the sort of party where there is underage drinking, but I guess I was wrong. I can tell that Zaidan, Ara, and Adelaide are just as surprised as I am; they hold the sort of look that I share with them.

"We'd better be heading home," Zaidan says hurriedly, and he lightly touches the small of Arabella's back, bids us goodbye, and heads out the door with her.

I feel sick. The last time I smelled the scent of whiskey . . . I don't want to remember it. I look around to make sure that nobody's looking. Then I quietly slip out the door.

Evidently someone has brought a stereo because on my short walk back home, I can hear a soprano singer with shitty pop music playing loudly. I also notice that Ms. Lillvik's car is gone, which explains why random teenagers would have the audacity to bring alcohol to the Lillvik home.

Sitting in my room with the door and windows shut makes the silence sound surreal, very clean, and almost unnatural. Mere minutes ago, I was surrounded by the buzz of loud laughter and small talk. Here, in this quiet place, I can hear the silence. It is a ringing in my ears, only just bearable. I lie down on my bed, relishing in it. That is, until there is a knock on my window.

"What're you doing here?" I say to Adelaide in shock.

"What do you think?" she says, hoisting herself on my windowsill. "I'm celebrating your birthday with you. You've finally joined us in the adult club." She points her hand, in a fist, at my face, pretending to hold a microphone. "How does it feel?"

"You should be at the most wonderful *alcoholic* party someone's having two doors down," I retort.

"Oh, shut up," she mutters. "Now let me in." She pulls a leg into my room. "I have rights."

"That doesn't mean you're allowed to enter someone's house without permission," I say, but I can't help but laugh.

"Sorry, I had to," she grins. "Bad jokes? Those are my thing."

"I'm not surprised."

When I know that she's safely inside my room, I turn away from her and sit at my desk. "I have a Lit paper to finish," I say blandly.

She walks over and grabs a pen and a piece of notebook paper. "And I have a Lit paper to start," she says nonchalantly. She sets her pen in between her fingers and writes her name with a flourish. "Due Monday, right?"

"Yeah," I say. "Nice play on words."

"Thank you; it's my specialty."

After a few of minutes of writing and hearing the scratching of pen against paper, I turn around to Adelaide sitting cross-legged on my bed, her nose almost touching the paper.

"What're you writing about?" I ask quietly. She jumps; she was evidently immersed in her work.

"What? Oh . . ." she says, slightly dazed by the impact of speaking to someone. Then the content of my question reaches her head. Her eyes light up. "Oh, I'm writing about the misogynistic tendencies of the Homeric poem *The Odyssey* and how it can antagonize feminism."

"Whoa." I am surprised that she's doing this topic. I turn my entire chair around. "So you consider yourself a feminist?"

Her brown eyes light up with a fire I've seen before: when she's particularly passionate about something. I brace myself.

"Firstly, I don't 'consider' myself a feminist, I am a feminist." I am about to apologize when she gives me a reply to that thought. "It's not your fault though; it's just the wording of your question."

She plows through her speech. "My concept of feminism takes a more egalitarian approach. Let's take an example, shall we? A girl wears a really short dress because she wants to impress a guy. If she doesn't actually want to wear the dress, and she's doing it because of societal pressures, then that's not okay. If this girl wants to wear the dress to impress her boyfriend and everything that occurs that night is completely *consensual*, then it's completely cool that she wears it. And if she just wants to wear it, is single, but wears it anyway because she knows she looks gorgeous and it raises her self-esteem, more power to her. Basically, all I'm saying is that a person should be allowed to do or wear whatever they want (provided it's legal) without fear of social pressure or consequences."

"Does that tie into the whole 'rape' topic?" I ask, interested.

"On that particular issue, I think we should teach people, regardless of gender, that rape is wrong, not to reprimand victims or potential victims about their attire. People these days blame anything but the rapist and I think that's disgusting."

"I completely agree," I say honestly.

"Anyway, what's your topic?" she says.

I chuckle. "It's not as in-depth as yours, but it's about the misogynistic tendencies of *The Odyssey*."

Fifteen minutes after Adelaide has finished her paper, I am only on my fourth paragraph. I'm just about to start discussing Odysseus's close call with the Sirens when Adelaide interrupts.

"Hey Troye, what's this?" Adelaide says curiously.

"What?" I say, tired and determined to finish my paper.

"It has your name on it," she says. I hear the crinkling of paper.

I whirl around and lunge toward the bed. "Don't!"

She drops the paper, which lies halfway open.

"Sorry," she says blankly, evidently confused. She picks it up, refolds it, and hands it to me.

"No, it's okay," I say. "You can read it."

"What exactly is it?" she says.

I take a deep breath. "So, you know my dad has his . . . problem. This is one of his suicide notes. He never went through with it, but it was a scary time for the entire family. We thought we were going to lose him."

"I . . . I can't read this," she whispers, her eyes wide.

"Please, read it," I ask. "I . . . I need someone here to know what it was like, living in fear."

"Oh, okay." Her voice sounds a lot stronger now, maybe even a little determined.

She starts reading the letter slowly, her hands shaking, struggling under the weight of words of hopelessness.

She looks at me with concern when she finishes it. "Why do you still have this?"

"It reminds me of how far we've come. Even though he's gone now, it reminds me that there was a time when things were far worse."

She doesn't answer me, but instead puts the letter back in its place.

"Is silence our adversary?" I ask tentatively.

"Yes, it is until you get your antimisogyny essay done."

I work. She grabs a book from my bookshelf, which I highly suspect is *Don Quixote*, and settles back on my bed.

"That's a good book, Adelaide," I whisper after a little while, not wanting to alarm her this time. "Have you read it before?"

She doesn't respond this time so I assume that she's too immersed in her book or she can't hear me. I decide not to repeat myself, and continue working on the conclusion of my essay. After thirty minutes it's obvious that Adelaide has fallen asleep. I confirm my hypothesis when I finish proofreading my essay. Her body is at awkward angles, yet she seems to be comfortable. I can hear shallow breaths from underneath the curtain of hair that has fallen over her face. Her eyes are closed delicately. *Don Quixote* is open on her stomach; she has almost completely finished the book. I gently pick up the novel, take the bookmark from my page, place it on hers, and shut it quietly. Then I reach out and shake her shoulders. "Wake up, Adelaide," I whisper.

She wakes up with an audible gasp, then relaxes when she takes in her surroundings.

"Hi," she mutters. I can still hear the sleep in her voice.

"I finished the essay. I know you're tired, so you should probably go home and get some rest."

She nods slowly and gets up with slow, static movements. She heads toward the window.

"You can use the front door, you know," I smile.

She shakes her head. "No, I don't want to be a bother." Before I can protest, she is already out the window. Just before her head disappears, she looks me in the eye and smiles.

"Happy birthday, Troye."

After she leaves I lie down. It feels nice to lie here after my back being hunched over a flimsy piece of paper that will determine my Literature grade. It feels comforting yet a bit painful to have my back straight. For the second time today, I relish in solitude. That is until, again, I hear the sharp rapping at my window.

I get up slowly and take my time, as I was almost asleep before the interruption.

"Hi," I breathe.

"Sorry," Adelaide says. "There are like six drunk teenagers passed out in my room. Do you mind if I sleep in your guest room?"

I shake my head. "No problem." I gesture for her to come inside. She clambers in, stubbing her toe in the process. "Shit," she whispers.

I walk her to the guest room, where she passes out almost immediately.

For the third time this night, I lie down in my bed and curl up under my blanket. The guest room is right next to mine, and both our doors are open. I can hear her shallow breathing. To the sound of her breath and the quiet buzz of silence ringing in my ears, my eyes close.

"Troye! Troye!" I hear hurried whispering.

"Mom, five more minutes," I hear myself saying.

"Troye! It's not your mom. It's Adelaide."

My eyes open wearily. "Whasthematter?"

"You've got to help me out. I've got to clean my room and the bathroom before my mom shows up."

"What time is it?" I mutter groggily.

"4:17 a.m., to be precise," she says brightly.

"Why isn't she home yet?" I yawn.

"Booked a hotel room. Needed some peace. Is coming home at exactly 6:15 a.m."

I would complain, but I have no choice.

Before I am even 50 percent awake I am scrubbing a toilet. It reeks of vomit and alcohol, two smells that I cannot stand. It is spotless in the bathroom now, but the odors linger. Adelaide walks in, presumably finished with cleaning her room. She scrunches her nose.

"It smells like crap in here," she says.

"Really?" I mutter sarcastically. "I didn't know."

"Give me a minute," she says. She bounds out of the bathroom and returns only moments later with a can of Febreze. She proceeds to spray every single inch of the room with the vaguely pleasant-smelling substance.

"Wait," I say, realizing something. "Where are all the kids that passed out in the room?"

"Oh," Adelaide looks at me for a second. "I drove them all home at about three a.m. I thought their parents would worry."

"That's . . . kind of you." I wonder aloud when exactly Adelaide woke up.

"Oh, at about two. There were things to be done."

I shake my head. "That means that you've had about two hours of sleep, correct?"

She nods in affirmation. "It's okay," she says before I can express my concern. "I've had three cups of coffee." She puts her hands on her hips, which is quite a feat since she's still holding the Febreze bottle. "Do I look tired to you?"

I shake my head tentatively.

She smiles warmly. "Good answer. Thanks for helping."

"No problem," I say.

She suddenly puts her palm on her forehead. "Crap," she mutters under her breath.

"I've completely forgotten about . . . I have to go . . ." She raises her voice. "You should come with me."

"Where?" I ask.

"Oh, just a room in the house," she says distractedly.

"To do what, exactly?" I question slowly.

She stops what she's doing, looks up at me, and grins. "Why, to meet Hades, of course."

I wasn't going to meet (to my utter disappointment) Hades, the Greek Lord of the Dead.

Instead, I was meeting Hades, the four-and-a-half-foot-long ball python, the Lord of Frozen Mice. He is majestic and not at all what I was expecting. He's docile, almost shy. I, a person who doesn't usually like anything that slithers, really like Hades, who at the moment is wrapping himself around my arms.

"I think he likes you." Adelaide smiles.

"So," I say self-consciously, very aware of the fact that there is a moving snake on my body, "you just have a snake in this house and pretty much nobody knows. And I've known you for months, and I just thought you were a normal, pet-less person."

"Is it a problem?" Adelaide teases. "Because if it is, you're going to have to leave the premises."

"No," I say quickly. "It's just that you have a fucking snake and you didn't tell me." I turn my head a fraction of an inch and smirk. "And I think Hades likes me more than you."

"Absolutely not," she insists.

She takes Hades from me, and sets him back into his habitat.

We stand there uncomfortably for a couple of seconds, and I take this as my cue to leave.

When I get home I don't know what to do. I pace from the window to the bed, up and down the stairs, and in and out of every room. When I grow tired of seeing the same environment over and over again, I start to exhaust another sense: hearing.

I tighten my bowstring. I play any scales I can think of. When I get bored of this, I pull out sheet music from one of my drawers. They are very old; the paper has grown brittle. I play the extremely simple, shortened version of *Ode to Joy* and other pieces like it. Then, I play sheet music that is significantly harder, things for quartets and solos composed by Vivaldi, Bach, and the like. When the stack of music is depleted and my fingers are almost bleeding from sudden overuse, I sigh and almost fall on my bed. Then, right before I put my viola away, I remember that there is one piece that I haven't practiced yet: "Enigma."

Wearily, I pull it out of my music binder. Straightening my back and standing up, I start playing quietly, and, unlike any other piece, I feel a connection to it. I still need to work on the high notes, but I can't wait to play it in front of an audience.

I play it over and over again, faster and faster until even my fingers have memorized the pattern of the piece. I play until I have hit every high note properly. I play until my pointer finger starts bleeding.

I pull an Adelaide and whisper "Shit!" under my breath. I walk briskly to the bathroom and open the cupboard under the sink. I grab a Band-Aid and wrap it snugly on my finger. The rest of my fingers, which are moderately calloused from years of practices, are red and rubbed raw. With this observation I decide to take a break. When I finally finish mourning the loss of a miniscule portion of blood, I rearrange all my sheet music and put my viola away.

Immediately after I have just finished cleaning my entire room, the doorbell rings. The sun is fading away, and Adelaide peers at me, her fingers tightly wrapped around the handle of her violin case.

"Hey," Adelaide says breathlessly.

"Hi," I say. "What's up?" I try to sound nonchalant, but my fingers hurt excruciatingly. It takes all that I have not to complain.

"Do you have anything to do?" she asks, almost timidly.

"No," I say. "Anything you need?" I squeeze my fingers behind my back to temporarily ease the pain.

"Well," she says, "I was wondering, would you like to practice 'Enigma' with me? I mean, we haven't practiced it in such a long time, at least together. And we've been neglecting it recently . . ." She looks at me, eyes wide, almost pleading.

"Oh . . ." I weigh out the advantages and disadvantages of saying no. In these spare seconds of the tension of her waiting for an answer, I notice she has her violin, sheet music, and a stand. "Okay," I say, almost already regretting the decision as my fingers are now throbbing.

When we get to my room, she looks at my open window and smiles. "I guess I should've just climbed in through the window."

"With a violin, sheet music, and a stand?" I raise my eyebrows.

She shrugs her shoulders. "Probably not, but don't underestimate me." She stares me down, looking for a challenge when there is none. When she realizes this, she stands a bit straighter, clears her throat, and promptly starts unpacking her violin. I do the same, but with much less vigor. I try my best not to wince.

"So why didn't you get in through the window?" I ask.

"Felt like I didn't need to give you a surprise."

"What a shame." I smirk. "I thought you were always full of surprises."

Before we can start playing, she studies my fingers. "Holy hell," she mutters, grabbing my left hand in both of hers. She grazes the raw skin with her fingertips until she reaches the Band-Aid. "What did you do to yourself?"

"Oh, um . . ." I rack my brain for potential excuses. "I'm an idiot," I conclude as a way of answering. I pull my hand away. "It's fine. I feel perfectly fine," I try to lie convincingly. "Let's just play."

I have a strong feeling that she knows that something is wrong with my fingers—you'd have to be oblivious *not* to—but she drops it.

"Okay," she says tentatively. She raises her violin. She gives the signal, raising the scroll of her violin just a couple of inches and then back to its normal position, and we start simultaneously. I avoid the excruciating pain in my fingers by focusing on the music, specifically Adelaide's part, as it is the only new part I'm hearing after playing mine over and over.

Adelaide has the melody first, her legato notes several octaves higher than mine. She is a tiny bit sharp on her highest note, and she expresses her frustration through an angry scoff. Then it's my turn. After several hours of playing just this part before, I handle it expertly. We continue through the entire piece and I'm proud to say I make no errors. This happens approximately three times.

"How did you do that?" Adelaide says in awe. "Have you been practicing?"

"A little bit." I nod.

"I feel like it's a bit more than a little bit," Adelaide notes.

"Thanks, I guess. I'll take that as a compliment." I put a tad of affected offense in my voice.

"I'm sorry for offending you, Troye *James* Washingturd."

"How do you—"

"—know your middle name?" she finishes my sentence with a smirk and picks at her cuticles. "Let's just say that your mother and I are on very good terms." She pulls her phone out of her back pocket. "She gave me her number. We talk."

"Please stop talking to my mother," I groan.

She grins evilly. "I've already reached stage three, which is embarrassing childhood photos."

I groan. "I hate you. How much have you seen?"

"I find it slightly adorable that you tried to eat a TV remote when you were four."

Perhaps it is fate that is my savior, or mere coincidence, but the doorbell rings.

"I'll get it," I say, completely forgetting that I have to get it, as this is my home. I fly down the stairs and answer the door. A cute dark-haired girl who looks about seven stares at me with her large eyes.

"Do you want to buy cookies for the orchestra at Cherokee Elementary School?"

She looks so cute that I can't possibly say no. I pull out my wallet. "Oh, all right. How much?"

I give her the money with a smile and in my peripheral vision, I see a ten-year-old girl smiling in triumph. I wave to her and she immediately looks panicked. I try to look encouraging.

"It's all right. I'm guessing you're in orchestra?"

She nods shyly. I gesture for her to come closer. She hesitates.

"I'm in orchestra too," I say. Adelaide pokes her head out.

"So am I," she says kindly. "What's your name?" She sounds confident and charismatic. So charismatic, in fact, that the girl saunters forward.

"Tai," she whispers.

"That's a pretty name, Tai." Adelaide smiles. "My name is Adelaide and this"—she points to me—"is Troye."

"Your name is pretty." She smiles back at Adelaide.

"Thanks," Adelaide says gently. "What do you play at school? I mean, what instrument?"

"I play violin," Tai says timidly.

Adelaide beams. "Me too!"

"Aw, you guys are the cool ones," I say, not actually believing what I'm saying, but hoping to make Tai feel more comfortable. "I play viola."

"I play viola, too."

Adelaide looks surprised. "Oh. That's cool. Not many people play two instruments. That's a gift you have."

"I play cello too," Tai states proudly. "And also bass."

"Wow," Adelaide and I say simultaneously.

"That's really impressive," I add enthusiastically.

"Thank you," Tai says modestly.

Adelaide bends down to the shorter seven-year-old's height. "And what's your name?" she says sweetly.

"Ming, but I go by Ming."

Adelaide grins. "Hello Ming who goes by Ming." Adelaide leans closer to the girl. "Do you like these type of cookies?" she whispers, all hushed, like it's a personal secret they're sharing.

Ming nods. "Yeah, but I can't have them 'cause Tai needs 'em."

Adelaide pulls a twenty out of her back pocket.

"Here," she says, putting the twenty in Ming's hand. "You can take this, and then you can buy your own cookies."

Ming looks at Adelaide in shock, then suddenly pulls her into a tight hug. "Thank you Addy-laide," she whispers into Adelaide's ear, trying her best to pronounce the name right.

"No problem, Ming who goes by Ming."

"Thanks for everything," Tai pipes up. "We have to go to the next house though."

"That's perfectly fine," I say. "It was really nice meeting you!"

In a few moments, we see the two girls walk down to the next house.

"Come on," Adelaide pulls me inside. "I still have to work on getting that high note right." She drags me up the stairs, an odd sight considering I am quite a few inches taller than her. When we reach the top, she inspects my hands again. She holds my wrist and points to my ring finger. "This one needs a Band-Aid too."

"Thanks," I say.

While I bandage my ring finger, Adelaide plays the measures that have the highest notes over and over again. Each time they get a little sharper.

She is on the verge of tears. "I can do it! I know I can!"

I tap her shoulder awkwardly. "Adelaide, I think you should take a break." She whirls around and I swear she's about to smack me in the face. Then her shoulders slump.

"You're probably right," she says.

I pack her things for her. "Come on," I say. "I'll walk you home."

"Thanks," she voices quietly.

It is a quiet walk to her house.

"Say hi to Hades for me. I'm sure he'll appreciate hearing from his favorite human."

"Oh, shut up," she says. I am relieved she says this; she sounds a bit like her normal self. "You only just met him today."

"Our friendship has no beginning or end," I announce dramatically. "It is everlasting."

She looks at me peculiarly. When she finally says something, it is this: "Keep your bedroom window unlocked."

Then she strides into the house, waves nonchalantly one last time, and shuts the door.

Adelaide

IT IS WRITTEN SOMEWHERE IN STONE THAT TROYE JAMES Saavedra, of all the people in the universe, has had the most unfortunate luck of coming across me. Why do I say this? Because it is precisely 12:11 a.m. and he is about to encounter a rude awakening. After my self-induced state of staying awake off of three coffees, he shouldn't expect anything less.

The first thing I notice is that he has a night-light. Six-foot-something Troye Saavedra is afraid of the dark. The boy in question must've kicked off his blanket during the night; it is heaped up, misshapen on the floor. His much-too-long legs are tangled, and so are his arms. I reach out and tap his shoulder.

"Troye," I whisper. "Get up. It's Adelaide."

He sits up, agile though he has just regained consciousness. "What do you need?"

"I got the high note." I grin as the realization of the time dawns on his face. "Yeah, I know, 12:15 and all, but it's necessary."

"All right," he says. "You're lucky that my mom's room is the furthest room from here and that she's a deep sleeper."

I pull a violin case out of this large black bag that has been draped across my back. I didn't bring sheet music because I've memorized the entire piece.

I start two measures before the highest note. I reach it with perfection.

Troye rubs the sleep out of his eyes, and smirks. "I think that might've been a little sharp."

I narrow my eyes. "Troye, don't you *dare—*"

He raises his hands in surrender. "Okay, okay." He smiles. "It was absolutely perfect."

I tiptoe and pat him on the head. "Good boy."

"Oh, so I'm an obedient animal now?" He mocks dissatisfaction.

I pat his head again. "It's okay; you'll get used to it eventually."

I start packing my violin. "Get some sleep Troye, if you can," I say. I proceed to climb over his windowsill and down the ladder. "Goodbye," he calls out when both my feet are planted firmly on solid ground once more.

I look up and wave. Then I begin the short journey to my own home.

A few days later, Troye is the most panicked teenager on the face of the entire planet.

"I can't do this. I really can't." Troye is pacing in the orchestra room, muttering profanities under his breath. In his uncomfortable state, he knocks over about three cellos in a domino effect. As the already anxious cellists glower at him menacingly, he speaks his mind. "Screw it. I'm not doing this."

I stop his pacing and put my hands on both sides of his head (which is actually quite easy because I'm wearing black heels). "Troye James Saavedra. Do me one enormous favor and shut up. You can do this." Troye looks up at the ceiling, obviously not believing what I'm saying. I force his head downward so he has no choice but to listen attentively. "You can do this," I reiterate slowly. "We can do this."

He nods shakily, and I remove my hands from his face. He has agreed to stop pacing, instead releasing his nervous energy by tuning and retuning his viola. While he finds solace in this, I change into my orchestra uniform, which is a long black dress that reaches my feet. After I have exhausted all other ways to spend my time, I do what Troye is doing: I tune my violin.

For the first time this year, we are not playing with the rest of the orchestra. It's fitting, Xavier says, because we are seniors. The cello and bass are doing their own piece as well.

We're doing several things that we never did in the past three years that I've been here. Firstly, we're doing this double duet thing where I play "Enigma" with Troye and the bassist, Idella, plays with the cellist, Prakash. They are playing an elegant piece named "Transcendence." Secondly, this concert takes place in January, while the concert used to be in December. There's also no program guide for this concert, which is slightly odd, but Xavier said that we didn't need to have one.

"Symphonic, get on the stage!" Xavier calls. "We're going to begin practicing in five minutes."

Troye has disappeared from next to me, but I assume he's gone to the bathroom.

"Adelaide, can you help the rest of the players tune? Or at least make sure that their instruments are tuned?"

I nod. "Okay." I walk away from backstage, headed for the orchestra room. Right before I step off the stage, I hear Xavier say, "Tell Troye too, if you see him!"

"I will!" I call back.

Little did I know that I would not be seeing Troye during the entire span of the concert, and that, for the first time in my orchestral career, I would attend a Rookwood High School orchestra concert but not play in it.

Troye James Saavedra was nowhere to be found.

Troye

I DON'T UNDERSTAND WHY PEOPLE CAN BE SO CALM ABOUT things like this. When I was younger, I'd see players at concerts play so smoothly with cool expressions on their faces. They never showed signs of panic or made any mistakes, as far as I could see.

My A string was tuned to perfection. So were D, G, and C. My bow was tightened, and it had enough rosin. I promised Adelaide I wouldn't pace, so, instead, I sit on a piano bench and tap my feet to no particular song or rhythm. A couple of people ask me to tune their instruments, and I do not object. In fact, I wish I'd taken more time tuning, as it would occupy my total attention and give me something to do other than worry.

After a couple minutes of poorly disguised panic, I decide to do what almost every bored teenager does: go on my phone. However, I do something I usually do which most teenagers don't. I check the news.

I find a recent article that looks interesting.

DRUNK MAN HITS TRUCK; IN ICU

Daily News's Jane Adams investigated a crash on the freeway a mere hour ago. A white Honda Civic drove head on into an eighteen-wheeler truck carrying furniture. The truck has a significant amount of damage done to its front, but miraculously, the truck driver was unharmed. The driver of the Honda Civic was not so fortunate, however. The man experienced several injuries to the head and the torso. "He was conscious right until the medics arrived. Then he passed out," one eyewitness says. One medic tells us that he had a significant amount of alcohol in his system. "No wonder he crashed," he says. The man has been taken to the Caldwell Hospital of Atlanta and we are currently awaiting reports from his attending doctors.

I finish reading the article, slightly saddened. I scroll down to the comments, searching for more information. Or perhaps an update on the man's condition. Then I see a top comment and decide to read it.

> *Bryan Fleming (6 minutes ago) - EDITED*
> *I was one of the witnesses of the accident. Right before he passed out, he said his name was Ivan Saavedra. If anyone knows him, please go to the Caldwell Hospital of Atlanta ASAP.*
> *-Bryan F.*

It takes me a couple of seconds to comprehend what has happened. When this happens in movies, really dramatic music comes on. The camera does a three-sixty-degree shot around the person reading the inevitably horrible news. There's a look on the face of the dramatic, larger-than-life hero that is indescribable. Trust me, that isn't how it works in real life. The only music I hear is the shaky, unsure sound of people halfheartedly practicing nervously. There are people laughing and talking, which adds to the underwhelming soundtrack. There is no camera in my face recording my facial expressions, and most likely to a casual passerby, an extra in the television drama that is my life, my expression hasn't changed. I probably look the same as I did five minutes ago.

I feel like pacing. But I promised I wouldn't. But I really want to. I pack my viola. I want to pace, but the concert isn't my main concern anymore. The startlingly calm conclusion I have made is simple: I cannot play tonight. Adelaide and I have worked so hard on "Enigma," and yet it has all been in vain. I put my viola back in its locker in the orchestra room's adjoining instrument closet. I pull off the jacket of my tux, now wearing just a white button-down shirt and black slacks. I leave it in the locker. I have no use for it now.

I do not pace. I walk. I walk all the way to the front of the school. The January air is still sharp. I quickly pull out my phone. I call my mom. She's at work right now, skipping my concert to support the two of us. I doubt she will pick up, but I hear her voice on the third ring. "Hello?" she says, confused.

"Mom?" I say shakily. Just like always, she knows that something is wrong by the sound of my voice.

"What's wrong?" she whispers, concerned. I can hear voices having a discussion behind her, and I also hear the clacking of keys.

"It's Dad," I say, my voice growing steadier.

I can hear her voice sharpen. "He hasn't shown up to your concert, has he? Is he bothering you?" For the past few weeks, my dad has been showing up drunk at places to confront me, but mostly to talk about my mother. "How's your mother?" he'd slur. I'd put a smile on my face just to piss him off. I'd say she was excellent, very happy. "That fucking whore," he'd mutter, and drive away in his Civic.

Her voice lowers even more, probably so her boss doesn't hear anything. "I can drive over and tell him to fuck off."

I am taken aback. Other than the night when I returned from the Tower, I've never heard my mom curse. She's been far more liberal after kicking out my dad. She smiles more, cracks more jokes, and is generally a lot nicer. Best of all, she has started treating me like an adult. It is exhilarating. However, I must focus on the topic at hand.

I chuckle hastily. "No, Mom; it's nothing like that. He's gotten himself in the ICU."

I know she's glad to be rid of him, but she still sounds worried. "What? How? Where?"

"He got into an accident . . . with a truck. He's at Caldwell."

She asks me another question.

I sigh. "Yes, Mom. He was drunk."

"What should we do?" she asks, leaving it up to me.

"I . . . I need to go. Now. No matter what, he's still my dad. Even if he's an asshole."

"And what about the concert?" she says calmly, completely ignoring that her only child has cursed.

I shake my head, even though she can't see it. "I can't play. Even if I don't go to Caldwell . . . I couldn't—I *can't* play like this."

"You really want to go?" she asks.

"Yeah." My voice is stable now.

"I'll come get you," she says firmly.

"Okay." I'm sitting on the curb of the side entrance, right outside of the cafeteria. "I'm on the side entrance."

"All right," she says. "I'll see you soo—"

Her voice is cut off by a deep, burly voice.

"Ms. Windsor? Are you talking on the phone?"

"Oh, sorry sir. It's just my son—"

"Is he in terrible danger?" The man's voice is sarcastic.

"No, it's just—he needs to—"

"Well, if he isn't in immediate danger, then why are you speaking to him on the phone?"

"He needs to—" She doesn't get to finish her sentence.

"This, however minor it is, is your first infraction. You will face consequences next time."

I hear the slamming of a heavy book. "You know what?" my mom protests defiantly. "I'm done. I quit. I have an eighteen-year-old waiting for me so I can take him to the hospital to see his dad. I honestly don't need any of your shit right now. I'm going to leave now—" I hear the rustling of papers. "And don't touch any of my belongings or my lawyer will give you a call." I hear the arrogance in her voice. "I don't care how high up you are in this business; your heads are stuck too far up your asses for it to matter."

I hear her pick up the phone. "Sorry you had to hear that, dear," she says sweetly. "I'll be on my way." She cuts the phone.

I can hear several parents' voices, people who are presumably walking to the entrance of the auditorium. Ten minutes later, I hear the clacking of heels and the thuds of heavy footfalls.

"Troye, why are you here? Isn't your performance soon?"

"What?" I look up and see Zaidan and Arabella. Zaidan is still wearing jeans, as usual, but he has attempted to achieve some sort of formality by wearing a blazer over one of his *Doctor Who* T-shirts. Ara is dressed in a long-sleeved royal-blue dress that ends right below the knees. She's wearing makeup, striking eyeliner making her blue eyes more noticeable.

I clear my throat. "I have to go," I say. "My dad's in the hospital."

Ara claps a hand to her mouth. "You have to go," Zaidan says. Then he speaks again. "Oh, wait. I guess that you're out here because . . ." I nod, urging him to go on. ". . . you're going to the hospital?" I nod vigorously.

"Did you tell Del?" Ara says suddenly.

For one second, I wonder who Del is. Then I realize that Del is Adelaide. I don't know why; I've always thought of Adelaide as Adelaide. Shortening her name seems like it shortens her personality. I shake my head.

"Oh, shit. I forgot about that. When you go inside, can you tell her that I can't play? Ask her to tell Xavier to play 'Enigma' with her."

Ana sighs, resigned. "All right," she says.

"I hope your dad is okay," Zaidan says plainly.

My mom pulls up in her gray hybrid Honda. "You ready?" she says. Her voice has fiery tones, just like Adelaide when she is passionate about something.

I pick up my book bag. "Let's go." I dump the bag in the backseat with a dull thud and plop into the front seat. The Caldwell Hospital of Atlanta is only thirty minutes away according to my mother's GPS. We don't talk, not because there is nothing to say, but because we don't need to. After twenty-five minutes, when the hospital is in sight, my mom talks to me, her throat raspy.

"Don't be so harsh." Her voice is soft but well-guarded.

"He doesn't deserve that," I say coldly.

"I know," she chuckles bitterly. "Of course I know!" She grips the steering wheel tightly with both hands, still facing forward with her head up high. "He's a son of a bitch, he is." She looks hollow, melancholy. I can't stand to look at her. "Did I tell you how we first met?" she asks.

I say no. "We were both at a college party. We were both drunk." She smirks a little bit. "Don't ever drink, Troye; the hangovers suck." She then resumes her story. "I can't remember all of it, just flashes. Next thing I knew, I was sick to my stomach in a bed I didn't recognize."

She looks at me for a second with a peculiar expression painted on her face. "I wasn't pregnant or anything, if that's what you're thinking." She laughs at my incredulous expression. "When I woke up, he said he was sorry and asked me on a date."

"He was sitting on the edge of the bed, waiting for me to wake up." She smiles sadly. "That was one of the good things about your dad. He'd never leave."

We are at a red light when she sighs, absentmindedly rubbing the spot on her left hand where her ring used to be. "I guess that's why he didn't just divorce me when he found Lavinia. He was afraid. He'd never done that before. Leave."

She shakes her head as if coming out of a trance. "But he's still a bastard, mind you."

I laugh. "I know, Mom. I know."

We pull into a parking spot without much difficulty. I stand up, my legs shaky. I stumble a little, but then start walking normally.

The hospital, like many others of its kind, is whitewashed. I hate it. It looks too pure, too clean for a building where the sick die and the healthy weep. It is horrible, inhumane. You'd think that a patient would be sick of white when twenty-four-seven they're worrying about seeing the white light that signals their departure from the world. It almost makes me laugh aloud, it's that amusing. But I don't. I hate hospitals. The coughing, the tired eyes, the sagging, and the worry lines are almost too much to handle.

I want to turn around and walk away. But I will not be like my mother, who runs from every situation she doesn't want to be in. Nor will I be like my father, who stays at the wrong times. But I'm scared. I gulp, take a deep breath, and walk to the lady clad in white at the front desk.

"Hello?" I whisper nervously.

She looks up from her paperwork and smiles warmly. "Hey sweetie. How can I help you?" She has a sun-weathered, round face and a deep, stereotypical Southern accent.

Encouraged by her kindness and hospitality, I speak significantly louder.

"Hi. I was just wondering if there is a patient named Ivan Saavedra here?" I take out my wallet and pull out a form of ID. "My name is Troye Saavedra, and Ivan is my dad."

I hand her my identification. She inspects it closely, looks up after a bit, and hands it back. "He's still in surgery. But–" she looks at her computer screen and clicks a couple of times. "I know that he will be placed in the S. Quagmire Ward, Room 4304. Quagmire's on the fourth floor. You can wait there."

I give her my thanks. Before my mother and I can head for the room, however, the lady asks another question. "Who is that with you, Troye?" she calls out.

"Oh." I put my hand on my mother's shoulder. "This is my mom."

She beams at my mother reassuringly. "Oh, all right." She suddenly looks sympathetic. "I hope your husband is okay, ma'am," she says sincerely.

In return, my mom gives her a tight-lipped smile. "No, Ivan isn't my husband."

"Oh," the woman says awkwardly, her face falling. In about a second, she regains her composure. "Well, dear, I hope he's okay either way."

"Thank you," my mother says stiffly and almost monotonously.

We walk away at an uncomfortably fast pace, zooming toward the elevators. We are surprisingly the only ones on the elevator.

"Mom," I ask softly. "You okay?"

She does what she always does: she gives me a melancholy smile and says that she is perfectly fine. Her eyes have a peculiar sort of sheen, like refined glass covering her irises.

The Quagmire Ward, unfortunately, is just as white as the rest of the hospital. The layout is not as open though. There are grandiose white-oak doors that line the white walls. Right next to each of the doors are small yet slightly obtrusive metal benches that narrow the width of the hallway. There are not any people sitting on any of the benches except one man. He is dressed in a too-large overcoat and brown trousers. He is hunched over, not necessarily crying, but wringing his hands worriedly. I pass him and sit down in front of room 4304. It is quiet for a long time, until I hear the turning of a doorknob. A small boy, who has sandy hair that brushes into his eyes and fair skin, shuffles out of a room. "Dad?" he asks. His voice is still high; it hasn't matured yet.

The man on the bench sits up and tries to smile reassuringly.

"Hey, little man," he says with a cracked voice. "How're you doing?"

"I'm fine," the boy says brightly. Then his face becomes upset. "Dad?" he repeats.

"What?" his dad asks calmly.

"Mommy's in pain," the boy says. "She's crying a lot."

The man's eyes start to water a bit, but he blinks the tears away. "I know, little man. She's hurting quite a bit. But that's not why she's crying."

"So why's she crying?"

"Little man, I think you'll understand when you grow up."

The boy pouts and crosses his arms. "But I want to know *now*!" he complains.

The man sighs. "You know how much your mommy loves you, right?"

The boy stands up a bit straighter and holds his head up higher. "Duh," he says eloquently.

His dad chuckles. "Remember a couple of months ago when we told you that you were going to have a brand-new friend to come live with you?"

The boy scrunches up his face, obviously trying to remember that far back. "I think so," he says. "Mom said that I was gonna have a sister or a brother." His face lights up. "When are they getting here?"

His dad looks pained. "They're not getting here, Reid."

"Why not?" Reid whines.

"An angel took him, or her, to Heaven."

Reid looks confused. "Why? Didn't the angel know that I was waiting for my friend?"

"The angel knew," he says. "But your friend wasn't ready to come down to Earth yet. That's why he took a trip back to Heaven."

Reid, no doubt still discontent with this answer, nods slowly. His dad releases a breath of air.

"Can you be a good boy?" his dad asks.

Reid nods again.

"Okay . . ." the man says. "I'm going to get some coffee so I can stay awake. Can you sit here quietly while I go get that?"

"Okay," the boy says. "Can you get me a cookie too?"

"Chocolate chip, little man?"

"Duh," the boy says.

"Be polite," his dad says sternly.

Reid nods earnestly. "Okay, Dad."

His footsteps fade away as he walks out of the ward. After about two seconds of silence, Reid starts swinging his legs back and forth. His left foot hits the leg of the metal bench with loud clangs. Then, for a second time, I hear the soft click of a turning doorknob.

A woman with long, straight, sandy hair who dons a billowing hospital gown peeks out. "Reid?" she says in a soft voice.

The boy stops his clanging and beams at his mother. "Hi Mommy!" She hobbles to the bench, much to the concern of my mother, but I elbow her gently as an indicator for her to let it be.

"Dad told me that an angel took my friend to Heaven."

The woman scrunches her face for a moment. "That's what he told you? That's exactly what he said? I mean, are you sure?"

Reid nods glumly. "Yeah."

The woman looks outward with a glazed expression on her face, as if she's thinking of what to say. "Reid," she finally settles on something. "Do you know what death is?"

"Dad says death is when someone goes to sleep and then they never wake up." The boy pauses. "Is that what happened to my new friend? Did he go to sleep in your tummy?" He looks at his mother's hospital gown.

The woman nods shakily. "It's something like that." She puts an arm around her son. "You know how I always tell you that life is precious?"

The boy says yes earnestly, wanting to hear more.

"Well, Reid, the thing is, life is precious because it ends."

"Why does life end?" the boy says inquisitively.

"Because life is a gift. But it's also a responsibility. And a burden sometimes," she laughs breathlessly. "God knows it's a burden." She pulls Reid closer to her and hugs him tighter. "But ultimately Reid, and never forget this: life is precious."

There is a silence that is neither an adversary nor a friend; it's just a spectator of the scene that unfolds before its eyes.

"Don't waste your life before you waste away, Reid. In your final moments, you won't want to have a really boring life flash before your eyes. You'll want to remember beauty, happiness, love, integrity, and bravery. Do me a favor, Reid. You fill your life with those things. Promise me."

Reid obliges. I feel my mom grip my hand and squeeze tightly, reassuring and comforting herself. For just a second Reid's mom looks into my eyes with a knowing look, a face of understanding and empathy. She nods briskly and I do the same.

Suddenly, we hear growing footsteps and Reid's mom gets up quickly, almost falling to the floor.

"Don't tell your dad I was here," she mutters urgently.

"Okay," Reid whispers, rushed.

His father returns, a small brown paper bag in a hand and a coffee in the other. He hands Reid the bag then tousles Reid's hair.

"Chocolate chip, as requested," he announces.

"Thanks, Dad," the boy says strangely, almost guiltily. Luckily for Reid, his dad doesn't catch it; he is far too busy drinking his coffee. We all look in the same direction when the stretcher is wheeled into the ward.

Lo and behold, there he is: my father.

I stand up suddenly, trying to get a better look at the man who has been tormenting me for the past few weeks. One of the people rolling the stretcher looks at me for a split second and says that he will be okay before disappearing into the room. Reid looks over from his bench and gives me a tentative wave. I smile weakly and give one back. Then I take a deep breath and walk into the room.

My dad is still unconscious, which spares me the trouble of attempting to make pathetic conversation.

"He's not going to be awake for a while," the woman that spoke to me a second ago says. "You have a long wait ahead of you."

"That's perfectly fine," my mom says in a scratchy voice, staring at my dad with an infuriatingly complex expression. The hospital employees leave the room and I am left alone with my unconscious father, my mother, and a cell phone as potential outlets to converse with or on. Of course, like any dignified teenager, I choose my phone.

When I turn it on, I see approximately seven missed calls from Adelaide, one from before the concert and the rest from the past half hour. *Oh shit*, I think. *She's going to kill me.*

I click the call button with hesitation. When it starts ringing I glance at my mother, who has taken a seat opposite me, and my father who lays sprawled on his bed, covered in bandages. I walk out of the room to talk to Adelaide. I see the familiar faces of Reid and his dad and wave to them inelegantly.

"Hi," Adelaide says, picking up almost immediately. Good start; she doesn't sound angry.

"Hey," I say nonchalantly.

"Is he okay?" she asks.

"Yeah," I say almost gleefully, relieved that she hasn't reprimanded me for missing the concert. Yet. "He's out of surgery, but he's still unconscious." After a moment, I add something to my sentence. "The complete moron."

"Troye . . ." Adelaide's stern voice is a warning sign.

"Sorry," I say quickly.

She sighs. "You shouldn't be." She clears her throat. "Where are you?"

"Caldwell of Atlanta," I say.

"Can I come?" she asks. "I'm at a party alone and I'm drinking as much water as a straight socialite drinking vodka at a gay bar."

I laugh aloud, aware that Reid is blatantly staring at me. "I assume that's a lot. And of course you can come. I need the company."

"Thank you!" she sighs dramatically. "I'm so bored. I've already planned five murders and nine kidnappings in my head." There is a long pause. "Hypothetically, of course," she adds hurriedly.

I smile even though she can't see it (although I'm sure that she can hear it in my voice). "Is that honestly what you do in your spare time?"

She sighs. "Actually . . . yes."

I laugh louder. "Adelaide, you can't make me laugh in a hospital."

"Sorry," she says simply.

"Okay, so when you get here, go to the fourth floor into the Quagmire Ward. You'll see me."

"All right." Her voice sounds a bit odd.

"Adelaide?" I'm slightly worried. "What is it?"

"Don't think I haven't forgotten that you didn't tell me a thing before you left to the hospital."

"Sorrysorrysorrysorrysorrysorrysorrysorry," I say in one breath. I hear Reid laugh.

"I'll accept your apology, but this isn't the last you'll hear of it." She cuts the phone.

I put my phone back in my pocket. I hear Reid speak.

"Is your girlfriend mad at you?"

I feel like I've heard him wrong. "What?"

Reid explains himself. "I asked if your girlfriend was mad at you. Because you look really young so you can't have a wife yet. But you can have a girlfriend. And whenever my mommy's mad at my dad, he says sorry a lot."

"She's sort of mad at me," I explain. "But she's not my girlfriend."

"Okay," Reid says, but I can tell that he doesn't really believe me. I ignore the deep need to explain myself and settle on sitting down and tapping my feet on the floor. I put my headphones in and hear the sound of 'Après un Rêve' by Gabriel Fauré playing. I smile. Adelaide probably put it on my phone. Ever since I met her, I've been listening to a lot more instrumental music.

She's here in twenty-seven minutes. Still dressed in the long black dress that is the female orchestra uniform, she walks surprisingly fast in heels.

"Hey," she says breathlessly.

"Greetings," I state casually.

Instead of asking about my dad, she does something unexpected. "How are you?"

I wasn't expecting this question, so it takes me a bit of time to answer her.

"Me?" I say. "I'm all right . . . I guess."

"Just all right?" She sounds personally offended by my statement. She rummages through her bag and pulls out a clear plastic box that contains the most gorgeous brownie to ever exist.

"Is that for me?" I breathe.

She nods. "I've already pre-checked the brownie; it doesn't have any pot in it."

I look at her oddly. "What do you mean by . . .?"

She shrugs. "It was a weird party. I had to check."

"Shall we go inside?" I say, pointing to the door.

She nods, and we both rise and walk through the entrance.

"Your girlfriend is pretty!" Reid calls out. Before he can say anything more, his dad hushes him with a smile.

"Not my girlfriend!" I call jovially.

"Sure," he mutters.

The scene is almost exactly the same as when I left it. My mom is sitting in the same chair, doing something on her phone. My father is in the same state as he was before, except the bandages splayed across his body look significantly bloodier.

My mother looks up. She stands and greets Adelaide with a warm hug. I note that this is odd because my mother is certainly not the most touchy-feely sort of person.

"Have you eaten anything?" Adelaide asks, concern etched on her face. My mom shakes her head. "Neither of us has."

"I could go get some Chinese," Adelaide suggests. "I know a place five minutes from here."

"That sounds lovely, dear," my mom says. "But all I really need right now is a good cup of coffee." She leans to the left to make eye contact with me. "Troye, will you go get some? It's just down the corner." She gives me that knowing *just do it* look with her eyes, so I decide—why not?

I walk out of the room, taking one glance back. My mother is speaking to Adelaide in hushed tones, smiling occasionally. Reid and his dad have disappeared from the bench, presumably in their family member's hospital room. I hear the echo of my footsteps on the bleached tile.

The snack room, thank the heavens, is thoroughly pigmented, the walls a soft brown the color of coffee beans. I see someone unexpected there: the receptionist from downstairs.

"Hey dear," she drawls while pouring a cup of coffee. "Did you see your dad yet?"

I nod. "Yeah, he's all right."

"Good." She sighs. "I wish they'd let me work longer."

"What?" My tone urges her to explain.

"I used to be a nurse here," she says. "The most ironic thing of all happened: the nurse, who comforted people every day about their illnesses, got cancer. Terminal."

"I . . . I'm sorry."

"It's fine," she says dryly. "I know that most people really don't know what to say. It's always 'sorry' or 'I'll pray for you' or just really uncomfortable silence. Don't worry; it's typical."

Having nothing else to say, I say sorry again.

She laughs. "You're not very typical even though you're saying sorry, Troye."

This reminds me of a vital piece of information I have forgotten to obtain. "Oh, I forgot to ask." I look at her sheepishly. "What's your name?"

"My name is Dan, short for Daniella." She looks unabashedly proud. "My mom hates that I've shortened it." She flicks a stray piece of yarn from her sweater into the trash can a couple of feet away.

"Dan, I don't mean to intrude, but why are you working if you're terminally ill?" Because she scoffs, I explain further. "I mean, why here? Aren't you supposed to be skydiving or traveling the world or something?"

"That's what a lot of people want to do, isn't it?" she thinks out loud. "Jump off cliffs and such?" She directs me with her next statement, sounding slightly frustrated. "You see, that's never what I wanted to do. My entire life is centered around here." She waves her hands around vaguely, almost knocking over a stack of coffee cups. "I don't really know what I'd do without it."

"Something less productive, probably," I say, taking a seat next to her. She leans her chair back and props her feet up on a coffee table. She shrugs her shoulders.

"I don't know. Anyway, after I had to quit, I asked if I could be a 'volunteer receptionist.' It's a lot more boring. There's not much work to be done. And they won't let me do any 'strenuous' activities. Plus, they give me short hours." She sighs. "I guess it's okay though. Better than rotting six feet under. That's not happening for the next eighteen months."

We hear the clacking of shoes and she rolls her eyes. "Not again," she hisses. "I wish she'd stop coming."

"Who . . ." My voice fades into nothing as I see a face I did not expect to see for the rest of the weekend.

"Well hello, Mr. Saavedra. I didn't expect to see you here, but I'm glad you've decided to keep my daughter company."

Mrs. Schroeder, with her smile through pursed lips and her cold, cruel eyes marches in, head high and back straight.

Dan groans. "Mom, why don't you ever just leave me alone?"

"Because," Mrs. Schroeder presses, "you need care and assistance."

"Mom," Dan mocks the word, "since when did you start giving a damn about me?"

I take the anger in her voice as a cue to leave. I grab the cup of coffee for my mother and start to walk out as slowly and as quietly as I can, trying to go unnoticed. Unfortunately, being extremely clumsy and more than six feet tall, I manage to be ridiculously loud.

"Troye, stay," Dan says firmly.

"Mr. Saavedra, I think it would behoove you to leave." Mrs. Schroeder's eyes narrow. "I believe my daughter and I need to have a discussion."

I shut the door gently behind me. Almost immediately I hear Mrs. Schroeder screaming. "Do you know how worried I am? You've driven me crazy! I can't sleep at night because of this! It eats me alive!"

Dan's voice is condescending. "Oh really, Mom? You've been worried? Is it you or me who's guaranteed to die in eighteen months? Is it you that's going to die after twenty-nine shit years on this planet?"

I have heard enough. I walk quickly to my dad's room, the scalding coffee almost burning my cold fingers.

"That took you a while," my mom says, her long fingers gripping the cup.

"You and I are going to go eat Chinese food. Then we'll bring some for your mom. Let's go," Adelaide announces jovially.

She exits the room with a flourish. My mom winks at me. "I got you a date," she teases. I roll my eyes and follow Adelaide out.

She pulls her car key out of her bag. I hold my hand out pleadingly for it. The response comes quickly. "Absolutely not!" She laughs evilly. "The inexperienced shouldn't drive."

"How are the inexperienced supposed to gain any experience if they aren't allowed to drive, therefore prohibiting them from gaining experience?" I challenge her.

"Good point," she notes. "But no."

"You suck," I mutter.

"Sorry," she feigns confusion. "What did you say to your *most generous* friend who's buying your dinner tonight?" She cups her ear with her hand, a smirk still playing on her lips. "My hearing is getting older with age."

"You're *eighteen*," I emphasize.

"Pain and difficulty are not defined by age," she retorts wisely.

"That was as deep as the Mariana Trench," I say.

She smiles and does a small curtsy. "My specialty."

When we reach the parking lot, I look for her run-down car. I don't see it anywhere.

"Where's your—" I stop suddenly when she pauses at a brand-new Mercedes.

"My dad decided to give me a gift for my senior year," she says sheepishly.

"I can tell why you don't want me to drive it," I say in awe.

"Yeah, well . . ." she trails off. I slide into the passenger seat. The new car smell fills my nostrils, making me scrunch my nose up for a second.

My entire life can be described as tidbits of interaction intermingled with copious amounts of time dedicated to awkward silences. A quiet of this kind is present now, sitting in the car with us, attempting to make conversation with us. I am sad to say that it has succeeded. Its form of speaking—silence—has been successful in shutting us up.

The Chinese restaurant, I am glad to say, smells a lot better than the car. The aromatic fragrances of warm food make my stomach growl. Adelaide hears the growling and she laughs.

"I know, I know. I'm starved."

"When was the last time you ate?" I inquire.

"Properly? Like an actual meal?" she asks. "Last night."

I'm flabbergasted. "*Last night?*" I repeat. "Adelaide, that was twenty-four hours ago."

She shrugs. "There was a concert today," she answers. "I can't eat anything before concerts or I might throw up from the nervousness."

"Understandable," I concede. "But still not healthy."

We sit down in a booth and talk. "How did the performance go?" I say casually. "You played 'Enigma' with Xavier, right?"

To my surprise, she shakes her head. "Xavier wouldn't do it. He said that he would push back the performance all the way to graduation."

The waiter comes over and takes our orders. We order an extra meal for my mother. After she has left, I return to the original topic. We talk while we eat.

"Really?" I ask. "That far away?"

"Yeah," she nods. "The next few concerts are themed, so the piece wouldn't really fit in." She leans on her elbow and takes a sip of water. "So Xavier talked to Pomeroy and *boom*: we're playing in front of the entire school." She gives me a knowing look. "Don't worry," she adds quickly.

I chuckle. "Adelaide, that's not going to help me feel any better."

"I know," she says smartly. "I decided to give it a go."

"Quite a pathetic attempt, I might add."

"I formally apologize, *Queen* Saavedra."

I smirk. "I thought that was Zaidan," I tease.

She points her chopsticks at me. "Not a chance," she says.

"And why not?" I ask.

"He's too . . . eh," she says cryptically.

"That explains everything," I note sarcastically.

"Doesn't it?" she states simply. She refuses to refute my arguments, and I refuse to change the topic, so we concentrate on our food instead. We are almost finished when I get a call.

"He's awake," my mom says. She cuts the phone.

I get up quickly and start packing food. "We've got to go," I say. "He's up."

She nods in understanding. She pays quickly and we exit the restaurant. We are almost back to the hospital when she asks what I think my dad will say to me.

"I have no idea." I attempt to speak nonchalantly. "Actually, can we just change the subject?"

"Okay," she speaks, never taking her eyes off the road. "Um . . . what's the meaning of life?"

"I actually know this one," I say.

"Well, what is it?" she asks impatiently.

I take a deep breath and answer. "Life is a gift and a responsibility and a burden," I squint, trying to remember Reid's mom's words. "Life is precious because it ends. Life is not to be wasted. Basically," I turn to Adelaide, "life is the most unpredictable, unexplainable thing in the entire world."

"Excellent answer." She sounds impressed.

"It's not mine, but remember it anyway," I say as we pull into the parking lot.

She pats me on the shoulder. "I will," she says genuinely. Afterward, she pulls open the door and leaves. "Hurry, Troye!" she says stubbornly, right before shutting the door.

I pick up the crackling bags of Chinese food and exit the car. My mother, rather than being inside the room, is sitting on the bench hunched over, sobbing.

"Mom?"

She looks up, her eyes red, her entire being contrasting the unpigmented hall. "Troye, go meet him," she sniffles. "I want to leave as soon as possible."

Adelaide sits down next to my mom and rubs her shoulders soothingly. "You can leave whenever you'd like," she comforts my mother. "I'll drop Troye home."

"Thank you, dear," my mom whispers, getting up and grabbing her car keys out of her trouser pockets.

"No problem," Adelaide replies. "Troye, go meet your dad. I'll walk your mom to the front."

They stagger down the hall, leaving me to Ivan Saavedra. The door is already open, and I strongly suspect that he has heard our brief conversation.

As I walk in, he coughs loudly. I can't stand the sound of it, but I don't know why. But then I realize: when my dad coughs now, he sounds like an old man. I start to feel sympathetic, but then he opens his mouth to speak.

"Your girlfriend's hot," he drawls lazily, staring anywhere but at me.

"Careful, Ivan. You don't want to get yourself into more trouble," I say coolly, even though I'm seething.

"Ivan?" he asks roughly. "Not going to call me Dad anymore? Have you stooped that low?"

"No, I've stopped taking shit from you."

"It doesn't matter anyway," he says gruffly, shifting in his bed. "You're no son of mine."

That stings, but I put a smile on my face. "Thank God for that. I'd be ashamed if you were my dad. You're a vile, sad drunkard."

I prepare to leave. I am almost out of his sight when he yells at me. "Tell me Troye, how many men has your mother spread her legs for since I left? Or women," he muses. "She always did bend to the will of everyone. I wouldn't be surprised if she was a dyke . . ." He laughs loudly.

I say nothing, turn my back on him, and leave.

Adelaide is waiting at the entrance of the ward. She knows something is wrong, which is not that hard, considering that my face is red and my fists are clenched.

"What did he say?" she asks immediately.

I shake my head. "It's not worth it, Adelaide."

She glowers at me. "What did he say?"

I sigh, giving in. "He said some stuff about my mom and emphasized how I was 'no son of his.' I told him he was vile."

I can tell she's furious. "What did he say about your mom?"

"Nothing," I say, already heading in the opposite direction. She doesn't take this for an answer. She grabs my arm tightly, forcing me to come to a screeching halt.

"All right, all right," I say, wriggling out of her tight grasp and holding both my hands up in surrender. "He was talking about . . ." I don't exactly know how to put this. What can I say, *Yeah, my dad just implied that my lovely mother is whoring herself around?*

"Yes?" Adelaide presses.

"He, uh, implied that my mother is . . . uh, *promiscuous*."

She turns a darker shade of red. Instead of telling me anything, she turns around and almost sprints into the Quagmire Ward.

"Adelaide . . . no!" I call after her, albeit not with much vigor; I am curious about what she is going to do.

She marches straight into the room, but not before angrily whispering to me, "Stay here!" I am genuinely scared of what the repercussions might be if I defy her. I listen to what she's saying from beside the door.

"Ivan Saavedra, if you had one ounce of dignity and compassion, you'd be one hundred—no, *one million* times the human being you are. I know that you've been through a lot, but that is not an excuse for you to slander your ex-wife like that. You're a wretched, horrible human being, if you can even amount to a human being. I am disgusted by you."

I can hear Adelaide breathing heavily.

"Sweetheart," my dad says with artificial sweetness in his voice. "Let's not focus on the negatives. That dress looks awfully nice on you . . ."

I hear a slapping sound and a sharp yell of pain from my father.

"If you want sympathy, you'll have to get it from Lavinia," she says coldly.

"You and your idiot boyfriend Troye stay away from me!" he bellows.

She marches out of the room, her head held high. "We will!" she yells, slamming the door behind her.

"Let's go," she says, fighting to keep her voice even.

"Okay," I say. "You all right?"

"No," she says. "But let's go anyway."

"Is there anything I can do?" I ask.

She tosses me her car key. "Drive me home."

"Really?" I say, dumbfounded.

"Just—don't ask. I might change my mind soon."

I shrug. "Okay."

The car still smells faintly of Chinese food, which, for some reason, is strangely comforting.

"Don't be offended—" Adelaide starts.

"—but you hate my dad?" I interrupt. "It's okay, because I do too."

"I was going to say that your taste in music sucks so I'm going to play my own, but yours works too."

"My music doesn't suck!" I say stubbornly. "You just have something against it because it has words."

She shrugs. "Words or not, I prefer my music choice."

She pushes some buttons on her car and plugs in her phone. Surprisingly, I recognize the piece. It's—

"'Caprice No. 5.'"

"I'm well aware," I say, pleased with myself.

"Congratulations," Adelaide says sarcastically. "Would you like a medal?"

"Actually, yes." I smirk.

Conversation dims when we are a few minutes away from our homes. "How were Idella and Prakash with 'Transcendence'?"

She claps her hands together. "Oh, you should've seen it, Troye. They were amazing!" She sighs happily in recollection of the concert. I pull into her driveway.

"Here we are," I say.

"I met Aaliyah," she says cautiously.

"The girl Xavier was talking to on the Tower?"

Adelaide nods. "She seems nice. And Xavier didn't seem as angsty as usual."

"That's good," I voice awkwardly.

"She seems polite enough," Adelaide starts to get out.

"She's his girlfriend, right?" I am unable to stop myself from being curious.

She laughs. "You really think that—oh my God—" She looks at me, obviously humored. "Can I have my keys?"

I get out of the car, then hand her the keys. "Who is she then?"

She looks at me with an odd sort of expression, and I know I will not get the answer tonight. "Never mind; good night," I say.

"Good night, Troye," she replies.

I expect to have a calm weekend to myself after the hospital incident, but what can I say? My life punches me in the face all the time. It gets irritating.

I have a fairly relaxing Saturday, studying for various tests and quizzes from the comfort of my bed. The only interruption to my evening without human interaction is a buzzing coming from my phone. Reluctantly, I get up and pull it off the charger.

"Troye?" Adelaide's voice, although fuzzy because of the poor connection, sounds decidedly normal. Subconsciously, I check the analog clock perched on one of my walls. 8:37 p.m.

"What's up?" I say, sitting in my office chair and propping up my feet on my clear desk.

"Can you come over?" The static behind her voice dims a tad and her voice sounds odd.

"Yeah, but what's wrong?" I ask, concerned. I sit up.

She sniffles. "It's just—what your dad said—I—I just feel so useless."

"Hey, don't let his words get to you."

"I know I shouldn't. It's just . . ." She breathes heavily. "Can you just come over?"

"All right," I say uncertainly. "Give me a minute."

"Thanks." She cuts the phone.

I open the door of my room and yell to my mother. "Mom, I'm staying over at Adelaide's!"

"Okay!" she hollers back.

I climb out onto the ladder and shut my window from the outside.

"That was faster than expected," her mother notes as she opens the door.

"Well, Ms. Lillvik, I do live two doors down." I smile.

Ms. Lillvik returns the expression. Then, unfortunately, it fades. "She's upstairs," she says cryptically.

"Okay," I reply with nonchalance even though I'm panicking. I have no idea what I'm going to do. I walk, with dread, up to the last room on the left.

The first thing I say when I open the door is "Whoa."

Adelaide chuckles. "I know," she groans, running a hand through her hair to smoothen it. "I'm a mess."

"No," I lie. "You're fine."

"Shut up," she says. She pats the spot beside her on her unmade bed.

"Come sit."

I take in my surroundings fully when I awkwardly slide my long legs under the other side of her covers. Her room, other than the bed and the desk, is as tidy as usual. Her desk is covered with several homework assignments, textbooks, and essays, both handwritten and typed. In the middle of the mess is a shut MacBook.

"I've been having an academic endeavor," Adelaide explains.

"Okay," I say, unsure of how to react.

"Did you eat dinner?" she inquires.

I shake my head.

She passes me a bowl and a fork. "Here," she says. "Do you like fettuccine alfredo?"

"That's fine, but how . . ." I don't finish my sentence. Adelaide pulls out a massive pot from beside her bed, struggling under the weight. "Here," she huffs. "Take as much as you'd like. There's a lot left."

I look at her in awe. She looks at me quizzically until realization dawns on her face.

"Oh," she says. "I'm emotionally compromised. And when I'm emotionally compromised, I eat fettuccine alfredo, lie down in my bed, and cheer myself up with some *Doctor Who*."

"I'm guessing that's what we're doing now?" I ask.

"If you'd like to accompany me," she says.

I shrug my shoulders and shift under the sheets. "Okay," I conclude. "It's been a long time since I've seen some *Doctor Who*."

"Then it's settled," she announces. "A night of fettuccine alfredo and *Doctor Who*."

"The best kind of night," I add jovially.

This is how we spend our Saturday night: snuggled in a warm blanket, eating food, eyes glued onto the tragic yet addicting adventures of the Doctor and his lovely companions. At some point in the night, her head is on my shoulder, her hair falling over her closed eyes. I am in an uncomfortable, slightly painful position. However, I don't want to risk Adelaide waking up, so I stay still. Ignoring the pain shooting through my shoulder and arm, I close my eyes and sleep, my last memory the faint sound of the television.

Adelaide

THE FIRST COHESIVE THOUGHT I HAVE IS THAT TROYE IS hogging the blanket. The second thought I have is that Troye talks in his sleep, speaking unintelligible babble to nobody in particular. Then again, that's what he does when he's awake too. I laugh to myself and sit up. I rub the sleep out of my eyes. Then, I decide impulsively, for the first time in ages, I'm going to put my glasses on rather than wearing contacts. I open the uppermost drawer on my nightstand and take them out. After putting them on (and blinking when I see the world a bit clearer), I turn to Troye. His hair is messier than usual and his arms and legs are everywhere, in all sorts of angles. His legs pin mine down, forcing me to wake him up before I can move. I pat his shoulder. "Troye," I whisper. "Get up!"

He groans and pulls the blanket over his head in one fluid motion, almost toppling me over.

"Troye, it's the morning. Get up!"

He opens his eyes reluctantly. He stares at me for about ten seconds, taking in his surroundings.

"Hi," he says finally, his voice all crackly and lilting at the ends. "You're wearing glasses."

"Well spotted," I say dryly. Then I smack him in the leg.

"Ow!" he yells. "What was that for?"

"That," I say, "was for kicking me at least twelve times last night. It's like you were running a 5K in your sleep."

"Sorry," Troye says unapologetically.

"Oh, shut up," I say, smacking him again. "I know you don't mean that."

I stand up and stretch my newly freed legs. "Let me give you some advice, Troye. There are two things you should never say if you don't mean them. Those two phrases are 'I'm sorry' and 'I love you.' Get it?"

Troye shuffles his feet awkwardly. "I'll keep that in mind."

"Sorry," I say, somewhat ironically. "Too intense for 9:13 in the morning?"

He nods. "Yeah."

"Let's go downstairs," I suggest. "We can make some breakfast."

We can smell eggs and pancakes as soon as we step out of my room. This isn't odd, I tell Troye, as my mom likes breakfast at about this time on weekends.

"What *is* odd," I observe, "is that it usually doesn't smell this good."

The final abnormality that I note is the sound of voices. We walk into the kitchen and find a scene that completely wakes both of us up.

"Hey!" Zaidan greets us jovially. "It's about time you woke up. We've been here since eight. We were going to wake you guys up, but then we saw how comfortable you were, so we decided to abandon that plan." He smiles cheekily.

My mother, Troye's mom, Zaidan, and Arabella are all seated at the breakfast table. Mrs. Markley is at the stove, which explains why breakfast smells so good.

"Good morning." Ms. Windsor smirks. "I would ask you how you two slept, but from what we know, you guys were plenty comfortable. I don't think I need to ask." She grins when Troye turns red.

"Mom . . ." he complains.

I glare at my mom so she gets the message. My mom speaks up. "Sorry, are we embarrassing you?" She lowers her voice to an evil whisper. "We've already placed bets on when Troye's going to ask you out."

"Troye, help a friend out and wait until the school year ends," Zaidan pleads.

"He's a broke man and he's desperate," Arabella laughs. I can't help but smile.

"Can we just stop this conversation now?" Troye mumbles. "It's really uncomfortable." He pushes his hands into his pockets.

"All right, all right." Ms. Windsor drops the subject, but still wears a self-satisfied smirk on her face.

"Good timing, because breakfast is ready," Mrs. Markley announces, taking a seat. "Help yourselves," she yawns. So we do. We all take a decent amount of food except Zaidan, who piles a mountain of breakfast onto his now small-looking plate.

"What?" he shrugs and holds his hands up in defense. "I've learned to appreciate food."

Ara takes a bite out of a pancake. "Haven't we all?" She smiles warmly at Mrs. Markley. "Thank you," she says. "The food is delicious, as always."

Mrs. Markley smiles. "Thank you, dear."

After eating, we all head upstairs while the mothers chat in the living room. I fall onto the bed, relaxing my body and sinking into the mattress. Next to me, Troye huddles under the quilt.

"Both of you look quite comfortable in the same bed," Zaidan teases.

"Shut up," Troye and I mumble simultaneously, not even bothering to look at him.

When I do look up seconds later, I find that Zaidan is holding his hands up in surrender. He and Ara take a seat on the edge of the bed. Ara has put one earbud in, now tapping her feet.

"What're you listening to?" I say interestedly.

"'Take Me To Church' by Hozier," she replies.

"Words?" I ask.

"Words," she replies.

I shake my head. "I don't understand why you have such a fascination for words in songs."

Ara smiles confidently. "I don't understand why you *don't* have a fascination for words in songs. It's a bit hypocritical. I mean, should Van Gogh have painted *Starry Night* in black and white just so people could have their own interpretations of the colors?" She holds out an earbud, indicating for me to listen to the song.

I sit up, rolling my eyes. "Don't be offended if I take this badly," I warn. "I haven't willingly listened to a song with words in years."

She smiles genuinely. "I don't think that that'll really be a problem."

"'Take Me to Church,' you said?" Troye pipes up. "Good song."

Ara thanks him dramatically, relieved that someone agrees with her point of view.

"Ready," she says excitedly. She hands me the earbud.

My initial reaction is that Hozier's voice is very low. It sounds nice, simultaneously melting into yet contrasting well with the music that flows rhythmically in the background. I am pleasantly surprised at the level of control that Hozier possesses over his voice. It's like having a steady hand while playing an instrument. I realize that I like it.

"So . . ." Zaidan asks in a voice that is octaves higher than his own. "What did you think?"

"It's better than I expected," I answer. I listen on. "Actually, screw that answer," I say. "This is actually fantastic."

Ara smiles widely. "What did I say?" she teases.

"See, Adelaide?" Troye smiles, popping his head from under the covers. "Not everything different from you is bad."

"That was as deep as the Mariana Trench." I smirk, using his words from a couple of days ago.

"My specialty," he retorts.

Zaidan fiddles with the TV remote. "You've been watching *Doctor Who?*"

"Yeah," I say nonchalantly.

"Don't kill me," Ara says cautiously, "but I've never seen *Doctor Who.*"

There are three simultaneous gasps in the room. I scoot back and sit with my back on the headboard. With another idea in mind, I shift to the center of the bed. I gesture for Ara to sit on my left.

"We're watching *Doctor Who* for Ara," I announce.

Zaidan scrambles for the remote. "Series one?" he asks.

I nod. By this time, Troye has already fallen asleep again, his head obscured by the blanket again. I lift the blanket up with much difficulty, as he has pinned it down with his arms.

"Exterminate!" I yell in his ear, using the catchphrase of the Doctor's greatest foe, the Dalek.

Troye screams in a high-pitched voice, almost unintentionally smacking me with his hands. To my amusement, he has managed to hit Zaidan with one of his flailing legs. Ara giggles, then gestures for Zaidan to come closer so she can give him a sympathetic hug. "There, there . . ." She ruffles his hair, patting his head soothingly. "It wasn't that bad."

He turns around and lies back down, his head in Ara's lap and his legs stretched out. He fiddles with the remote and the first episode of series one starts. I get out of the bed and shut the blinds, darkening the room. Then I squeeze back in between Troye and Arabella, carefully avoiding trodding on Zaidan's legs.

We all watch silently, other than Zaidan. Ara hits him lightly on the shoulder to shut him up whenever he decides he wants to recite the lines of the actors two seconds before they actually say them.

"Shut up," Ara finally hisses. "You're ruining it for me!"

The horror of interfering with someone's first *Doctor Who* experience gets to Zaidan. He remains silent for the duration of the next three episodes.

Ara's cell phone rings. We pause the fourth episode so she can talk in peace.

"I've got to go," she says nonchalantly. "My mom called."

She pats Zaidan's hair, indicating for him to get up. She slides her phone into the back pocket of her jeans.

"Zaidan, drop me off at home?" she asks.

Zaidan rolls himself off the bed. He attempts to pat his hair down; it was mussed up by Ara running her hands through it for the past few hours. He fishes his keys out of his front pocket. "Let's go," he says.

Arabella

I CAN'T SAY THAT I'M SURPRISED WHEN SHE CALLS. I LEFT HER a note, but I doubt that it matters.

"Arabella." Her voice is cold and monotonous, the way it gets when she's angry.

"Mother," I say formally. Zaidan always makes fun of me for speaking to her like this.

"It's like you're setting up an appointment with her," he'd say.

"Where are you?" Her voice is somewhat calm, which is a good sign.

"I left a note," I answer. My response agitates her further.

"Arabella . . ." she warns.

"I'm at Adelaide's house."

"Why is your car still in the driveway?" she asks suspiciously.

"Zaidan picked me up. Ms. Lillvik invited us to breakfast."

"Okay," she says cryptically. She seems to have accepted the fact that I have left the house without asking for permission.

"So . . ." I am slightly unsure of what to say.

"Come home," she says.

"All right," I say, fighting to keep my voice even. "I'll be there soon."

Without responding to me, she hangs up.

I ask Zaidan to take me home. We say our goodbyes to Adelaide and Troye. Zaidan holds open the passenger door of his car and gestures for me to sit inside. I thank him and he bows ridiculously low.

"No problem, Your Majesty," he announces right before shutting the door. He hops into the driver's seat, a wild look in his eyes.

I look at him oddly and gesture to him. "What are you all worked up about?"

"I love driving," he states. "It makes me feel important."

I look at him, slightly irritated. "You are important," I say, sounding cheesy yet honest.

He merely shrugs his shoulders. The most impossible task in the entire world is trying to get someone to understand they are amazing, especially if their self-esteem is low. Whenever Zaidan feels like he's not important, I want to grab his shoulders and scream at him that he's the most important person in the entire world. I want to tell him that his self-esteem should be as high as the Burj Khalifa because he is worth more than any precious metal on the planet. It frustrates me that I am utterly useless when it comes to these matters.

I know he hurts. Believe me, I know. When you meet someone so fantastic, you want any negative emotions to be intangible. You will put yourself through anything to keep things that way. That's what Zaidan does. He sacrifices his own emotional stability so he can provide support for others. To him, everyone is important except himself. I hate that he thinks that way.

As we approach my house, I feel an impending sense of dread. It reminds me of my ballet lessons as a child. I hated the instructor, Miss Jeannette, who thought it was amusing to humiliate as many students as possible in the time span of one session. I hated going there, dreading every second of the ride to the lesson and the lesson itself. When I voiced my opinions to Zaidan, he sneaked me out for a few weeks to go sit at the café a couple of blocks away from the studio and sip tea in peace. That is, until we got caught. My mom acted distant, not reacting much but removing me from classes anyway. Nevertheless, I was happy to get out of there.

"Here you go," Zaidan says, pulling into my driveway. "Need anything else?"

I shake my head. "No, it's fine." I take off my seat belt and lean over and give him a hug and a quick peck on the lips. "Thanks, Zaidan," I add.

"You okay?" he says. "I mean, are you going to be all right?"

I nod, probably unconvincingly. "I'll be okay."

He kisses me again. "Tell Logan I said hi," he says.

"I will," I promise to him while getting out of the car.

"Love you," he calls before I shut the door.

"I know," I say. "Bye."

My mother opens the door even before I reach the doorstep. She nods briskly at Zaidan, who has become slightly redder, coming to the conclusion that my mother has seen us kiss. He gives her an awkward wave, smiling at her sheepishly. I give him a final wave, then watch as he pulls out of the driveway and turns around the bend.

My mother's nails are always manicured, long red talons likened to those of a Fury's from the depths of the Underworld. My dad, during small chats at the dinner table, has expressed on several occasions that he hates them. A conversation about this would go something like this:

"It's too unnatural," he'd say.

"I like it," she'd snap back fiercely. "What are you trying to insinuate, Barrett?"

My dad would give out a resigned sigh. "Nothing, Marie. You can do whatever you'd like."

"Like hell I can," she'd say through a mouth full of food.

It is with those same talons that she grips my arm and leads me inside.

"Mom, you're hurting me," I say in a low and cautious voice. She doesn't seem to care very much.

"Thank whatever the hell you believe in that your father isn't home yet." She pushes me toward the stairs. "Get upstairs and don't come down until I call you for dinner."

I decide that I'd better not respond with a scathing remark. And, perhaps, it is better if I don't clutch the marks her nails have carved into my skin. As I tread slowly up the stairs—any sudden movements might trigger one of her fits of rage—I can hear her storming into the dining room.

"Stop that racket, Logan!" she hollers.

I hardly noticed that Logan was playing the piano; I've gotten used to it. Logan ceases playing immediately. I can see why she heard it from the dining room. He was playing a very loud piece. He's been playing music like that recently. Whenever Dad gets home, he and Mom get into plenty of rows. However, I think the only thing my mother seems to love more than yelling at Dad is yelling at me. Logan plays these loud, fast-paced pieces because he wants to drown everything out. He is not a runner or a warrior; he can't run from or fight against any of his problems. He drowns them with music instead. I don't know exactly how I feel about this, but I'm glad he's not drowning them with alcohol.

I open the door to the opening notes of what I recognize as the first movement of Beethoven's "Moonlight Sonata." Logan looks up from his sheet music for a millisecond to give me an understanding nod.

I lie down on his unmade bed. I suddenly recognize that I am exhausted. I know I shouldn't sleep, so my mind wanders as I stare off into space.

When I was nine, my parents had the biggest argument imaginable to an elementary schooler. Looking back on it, it was really petty, something about which one of them would pay one of our car's repair bills. My dad took me out of the house, sat me in the car, and drove away from the glittering lights of our neighborhood.

"Where are we going?" I asked my dad, who I distinctly remember gripping the wheel loosely with one hand.

When he spoke, his voice was as soft and as fragile as a feather. "We're going to the park," he whispered. "I'm going to show you some stars."

I was excited about finally having a proper sort of adventure with my dad, despite the circumstances. It was almost midnight and the park was deserted. The scent of freshly mown grass and clean air lingered. The moon was full and bright, casting an eerie glow on everything.

We climbed up onto a large artificial rock whose sides were used for rock climbing in one of the playgrounds scattered across the entire park. The surface of the top of the rock was flat, though the sides were bumpy and difficult for a nine-year-old to climb. It wasn't much of a view when you looked forward and all around you, but the scene changed altogether if you looked up. The sky was cloudless and the park was isolated from other buildings of the area. All was dark, so there was no light pollution that obscured our vision of the glittering specks in the sky.

We stretched out and stargazed.

"What's that one?" I murmured, pointing to a particularly bright star.

"That one?" my dad said, reaching his hand out as if to capture the star.

I nodded. "What's it called?"

"To be honest?" my dad said. "Not a clue."

I giggled.

"I was never taught about them, you know?" he said thoughtfully. "My daddy thought that stars and astronomy were a waste of time. Didn't bother with them at all."

"Well, why didn't you just Google it if you were curious?" I asked.

He chuckled heartily. "We didn't own one of those fancy computers you kids have nowadays. Besides, my old man told me not to worry about them. So I didn't."

Reminiscing on these final words, I fall asleep in Logan's bed.

"Ara! Dinner!" Logan shakes me awake.

"Fine," I mutter. "I'm getting up!"

It's a long walk downstairs. Logan is jittery, leading the way down the stairs. My hair's a mess and my eyes are red from the sleep. She's probably going to think I've been crying. Nearing the "fuck it" mentality, I sit normally at the table, not daring to look up.

"Hey, Ara." My dad's low voice emerges from the fog of tension that is currently settled in the room.

"Hi Dad," I say quietly, focusing on eating as quickly as I can so I can leave as soon as possible.

"We're all gonna have a family night," my dad announces jovially. "The four of us, some snacks, and a movie." He beams. "How does that sound?"

The rest of us don't say anything, but we do give him non-committal nods.

"Then it's final," he grins, piling his plate with food.

We say nothing. This proves to be partially good because my mother has no time to complain about my absence this morning, though she does glare daggers at me through dinner.

When we all finally settle down on the various mismatched couches and armchairs in the living room, my dad turns on a movie. To me, it is nameless and uninteresting. I can see that Logan is evidently bored. He is tapping silent rhythms on the coffee table with both hands, not paying attention to the movie.

Halfway through, my parents both laugh loudly. I stare at them, contemplating their relationship. Sure, my dad's hand is wrapped around my mother's waist right now and her arm is around his shoulders, but does Dad love her? I don't really know what love is. Even so, I know that I love Zaidan. Or do I? I don't know. Zaidan has said that he loves me loads of times, but I've avoided saying it back. I don't know why I can't say it to him. Perhaps I don't believe in love. Maybe I just can't decipher it.

Looking at Zaidan's parents, I can tell that they have a stable relationship. I'm smart enough to tell that there's an anomaly in my parent's relationship. If not anything else, wouldn't it be love that is the issue?

Once, on another trip to the Rock, my dad admitted to me that he had only wanted one kid.

"What about Logan?" I had inquired. "Why'd you have him if you only wanted one kid?" After a moment of silence, I had decided to better explain the question that I had posed.

"Because he's the second child, and that's two kids," I explained eloquently.

My dad sighed. He had started to do that a lot. "Your mother wanted a baby boy to call her own," he said. "She told me that she was gonna get a baby boy, whether or not I gave him to her."

I was too young to understand the impact of what my dad told me.

He had shrugged his shoulders. "So I gave him to her. Looking back on it, I don't regret it at all now; Logan's a good kid."

To me, it didn't matter whether or not he liked Logan now. What I was concerned with was why my mother had made him have another kid even though she knew he didn't want another one. The only thing I understood at the time was that making others feel uncomfortable or sad was inherently wrong.

When I was younger, I would hear stories about love. The couples would either get along well or, when they didn't agree on something, they would work it out though a civil compromise. Couples on TV didn't argue with beer bottles in their hands or through vicious screaming matches. I knew that my parents and their relationship were topsy-turvy and dysfunctional, but I never really understood why. Now, after many years, I have come to this startlingly simple conclusion: maybe it was the lack of the ever-elusive, intangible love.

What pulls me out of my own thoughts is my mother laughing loudly. This time, she points at the actress on the screen.

"She's quite fat," she states. "It wouldn't hurt to lose ten pounds, don't you think?"

My father looks uncomfortable and Logan and I look at each other with knowing looks.

We both hate this sort of blatant, discriminatory misbehavior. Logan looks like he's about to say something, but then he closes his mouth, still looking furious. I am filled with an indescribable rage. Looking at my own brother so angry yet helpless makes me do something extremely reckless.

"It doesn't matter if she's more curvaceous, Mom. At least she's doing something with her life, unlike the four of us. She's starring in a movie, probably getting awards, and just embracing herself. She doesn't need to lose ten pounds; she's empowered and gorgeous at the same time."

My mother's eyes widen in shock, and then narrow in anger. "I can see that you still haven't humbled up after your little escapade this morning. And you obviously haven't heard of the tons of tabloids that make a living off these kinds of things. If she wants to put herself on a screen in front of millions of Americans, she's going to have to expect the criticism. There's no need to be such a bitch about it."

"Just because some trashy tabloids talk about people doesn't mean that you should. That means that you share something in common with them: being *pathetic*."

Before my mother can react (which would probably be by hitting me), my dad gets up.

"Come on, Ara," he says hurriedly. "We're going to the park."

"No; it's fine, Barrett." My mother's voice is cold. "If her *dignity* and *intelligence*"—she spits as if the words taste rancid—"take her away from us and her values, so be it."

"You know what?" My father's voice raises. "Maybe leaving this goddamn shithole of a family will be better for her than anything that we're doing."

I can tell that this is the beginning of a particularly nasty argument. I can see Logan sliding slowly toward the stairs, also aware of the oncoming storm. I turn my attention back to my mother when she starts speaking to me again.

"I can tell that nobody ever showed you how to respect your own mother," she says to me, trying to make me feel guilty. I want to cross my arms. Evidently, it's not working. It's good that she keeps her attention on me. From my peripheral vision, I can see Logan halfway up the stairs, doing a good job at making no noise.

My mother then turns her attention to my dad. "I guess you're right, aren't you Barrett? Ara should've been born in another family, right?" She puts a hand on her hip. "She needs a family that actually understands her shitty problems, right?"

She has a wild look in her eyes, almost menacing. I have never been more scared in my entire life.

"Aw, your baby girl cuts herself. How *sad*." She has a condescending tone. "Do you know how much shit I've had to deal with in my life? And what a high fucking pedestal you've kept this girl on?"

My eyes water. No matter how much you try to convince yourself that you don't care, when anyone says things like these, especially your own mother, it hurts. I want to be impermeable, to have thick skin. I hate when people see me cry. It makes me look weak. Goddammit. I resist the urge to wipe the tears from my face. Extra movement will attract her attention, and she will mock me for it.

Unfortunately, the strategy of staying still does not go unnoticed by my mother. She turns to me, her eyes wide.

"Oh, she's crying now?" My mom laughs bitterly. "Please, cry some more."

I stay still.

"Come on," she says forcefully.

I wipe my eyes, unable to stand it anymore.

"No, no, no!" She sounds frustrated. "Cry more. Go ahead, before I bust out the popcorn."

My dad grabs my arm and leads me to the front door. I slip on my shoes. "Come on," he says in a low voice. "The Rock."

This is how we leave that night, both of us silent as my mother throws obscenities at us before slamming the door shut.

"I have school tomorrow," I say. "We've got to come home eventually."

He shrugs the problem away. "Doesn't matter," he says.

The drive to the park is punctuated by silence, which isn't abnormal. My father and I have had several conversations in which the main speaker is silence. We relish in it. It is more comfortable to say nothing than make useless conversation. A picture holds a thousand words, people say. Silence holds a million.

We don't speak as we settle down on the Rock. Unlike the first time we visited, there are no stars visible; they are obscured by wispy clouds. Instead of speaking, we think. I don't know if the moral code of the universe permits a child to hate her parents. They've raised me, but does that matter? They've done a shitty job. I don't know if I can hate my parents, but that look in my mother's eyes, the hateful things she said, they come flooding back to me. How can someone who loves her kid say something like that?

I used to think that no matter what, my parents always knew what was best for me. After growing up and seeing their constant fights, I'm not so sure anymore. Maybe the one who knows what's best for me is me.

I stare at the gray clouds that drift along in the starry sky. Lying there almost makes me feel content.

My dad taps my shoulder. "Sorry about what she said," he says.

"It's okay," I say in a strained voice.

"We should head back soon," he suggests. "She'll be worried."

I scoff. He ignores me.

When we get home all the lights are off downstairs. My mother is asleep. This is good; she won't yell at me until tomorrow after school at the earliest. Or, if I'm almost impossibly lucky, not at all.

I am too tired to do anything but sleep. Picking up my backpack, I tiptoe up the stairs, cringing every time I hear a creak. When I finally reach my room, I dump my bag on the floor, regretting it almost immediately when a loud thud reverberates around the room. Not bothering to change out of my school clothes, I crawl into bed.

It is the feeling of doing nothing that sets me off. Horrible, twisted strands of regret and pain and suffering. Lying on my bed, wondering what I could be doing instead of wondering. Agony races through my veins, filling me with a hollow, numbing feeling. There are musicians playing in front of an infinite number of people. There are authors sighing happily as they finish the last paragraph of a story that never ends. I am lying on my bed, wondering.

I have a knot in my stomach that grows tighter and tighter, unable to alleviate my restlessness. I want to go for a walk in the freezing cold just to think. But that is the sole thing that defeats me—the damned thinking, the pondering of how insignificant my life is. The curfew set by my mind has no effect. Restlessness. Pain. Unease. I am not satisfied. I don't know if I am anxious or stressed or tired.

As the white noise of whatever is playing on my phone doesn't subside, I grow frustrated, not with anyone else but myself. *Am I depressed?* I think to myself. I know the answer, but I wish I didn't. Candlelight guides lost souls and mourning hearts, but get too close and it burns you up. My eyes widen in fear as instead of flames, thoughts engulf me. Life is full of demons, I think, but I have no demons other than myself. These demons come out at midnight when I have no one else to talk to.

I do not want to be depressed. I am frustrated and angry and tired and restless and indescribable. I am doing nothing. And I am not happy.

Sighing, I get up. I turn to look at my clock. It is 1:52 in the morning. I turn on my bathroom light and open the right door of the vanity. My mother has left a note there, along with a box. *Use if weak*, it says. The box contains a single razor.

I sigh. I am weak.

Adelaide

THERE IS A MOMENT WHEN YOU SEE SOMEONE'S FACE AND realize something is wrong. It is a juncture of impending doom: a split-second decision. Will you choose to ignore it and to act if nothing has happened? Or rather, will you take the route of thorns, ask what's wrong? The second is tedious, a cacophony of wrong decisions ringing in your ears if you make one incorrect move, get cut by the thorns rather than reach the crimson rose.

In this case, I say screw the roses and the thorns and the choices. When Arabella shows up to school on Monday, today, not wearing an oversized sweatshirt and leggings, I know something is wrong. Ara always wears oversized sweatshirts and leggings, except when something is amiss.

At first, it wasn't on purpose; Troye, Zaidan, and I figured it out eventually. When she noticed it herself, she started using it as her official coping mechanism.

Those days, like today, she goes all out with her clothes. She wears a blazer and does her makeup (which she rarely does) and acts important and all-powerful. But if you look observantly, you can look past the façade, see the utter brokenness and the jagged pieces of melancholy madness.

This is the hard part about trying to fix a broken person: you must be cautious not to cut yourself on the pieces. You dare not shatter yourself to fill in the missing pieces of someone else's glass walls.

Thankfully, I know this is not the case with Ara. Unfortunately, I do know that the only thing binding her together is the meager tape called willpower. She is about to break. Or worse, she is covering the cracks with tape, hiding the scars with long sleeves and an artificial smile.

Ara and I walk wordlessly to the closet that contains the school's instrument lockers. It's a regular thing. We both arrive at school about an hour before other students. Xavier always leaves the second (and rarely used) door unlocked. We sit in a corner of the closet, silence creeping in from the cracks under the door.

She rests on a wall, inches from a broken bass. I sit next to her.

"What's wrong?" I say immediately, my voice scratchy.

"Nothing." She lies well.

"Bullshit." I face her. "What's wrong?"

She looks at me, almost terrified. I back off. "Sorry." My voice is softer. "You don't have to tell me."

We do not speak. When she leaves after about half an hour, claiming to need to attend a study session, I say nothing. I have never felt more useless.

The rest of the day is spent doing nothing. Every sound takes a backseat, mere white noise to my thoughts. The only thing that snaps me out of my daze is Literature. We are finishing *The Odyssey*. Now, like every other generic Literature class, we have a discussion to tie all the loose ends and answer all lingering questions.

"Mrs. Vaughn?" A guy with a deep voice who sits in the back of the class raises his hand lazily, his hair messed up and an indifferent expression plastered on his face.

"Yes?" she says eagerly, excited that he is contributing something to the conversation for the first time. "Would you like to add anything, Nathaniel?"

"Yeah," he says uncertainly. "I want to ask a question."

Most of the students are paying attention, suddenly interested.

"Um," he opens up his shiny, rarely used copy of *The Odyssey*. "So . . . when Eurymachus talks about Penelope tempting the suitors, doesn't he have a point?"

Before he can go on, there are murmurs of dissent and agreement from the rest of the class. If you look closely, you can see that almost every girl in the classroom has stiffened. Mrs. Vaughn silences the class, a calculating look in her eyes, determined to hear him out.

Silence Interrupted

"I mean . . . if a girl wears tank tops and a short skirt, shouldn't she . . . you know . . . expect guys being attracted to her?"

There's an uproar. The girls are angered, and some of the guys are nodding in agreement. The girl next to me drops a note in my lap. It's from Mrs. Vaughn.

Don't overreact, it says. *Go easy on him. Be merciful.*

I look up at her and she smiles at me.

I raise my hand. After the school heard about the whole "Invictus" thing last semester, it is no surprise that people are looking forward to what I'm going to say.

"Adelaide," Mrs. Vaughn sounds amused. "Anything you'd like to say?"

"May I go to the restroom?"

The entire class seems to sigh in disappointment at once.

"Um . . ." Mrs. Vaughn looks surprised. "Okay?"

I get up, glaring at Nathaniel, and walk out of the classroom. I go down the stairs and head out toward the parking lot. I double-check to make sure the blinds are drawn in Mrs. Vaughn's room.

I pull out of my parking spot and drive home twenty miles over the speed limit. At home, I grab something quickly and then head back to my car, the driver's door still open and the keys in the ignition.

When I am back at the school, it has only been about fifteen minutes since I have left the class. The girls and a few boys are on one side of the classroom, furiously arguing with the other side composed of all males. They take no notice of me entering.

"That took a while." Mrs. Vaughn raises her eyebrows.

"The closest bathroom wasn't working," I lie fluently. "I went to the one at the front of the building. And I picked this up from a teacher's class, if you don't mind." I show her the object in my hand. She stares at me inquisitively, then seems to let it go.

"That side"—she points to the majority of girls—"is defending Penelope, while that side"—she flicks her hand to the other side with an obvious scowl of disapproval—"has decided that the suitors were justified. Pick a side."

143

"Um, actually," I say cautiously, "would it be okay if we went back to a seated discussion? I'd like to make a point."

She nods.

"And also," I ask audaciously, "would you mind if I left this on the desk for now?"

"Sure," she shrugs. "And I must say that it is quite pretty."

I smile. "Thanks." I take my seat.

"Guys, get back to your seats!" she calls out. "We're going back to formal discussions." Even though Mrs. Vaughn looks like she can't be a day over thirty, people take their seats. We know that if we disobey her, there are consequences. She is powerful yet friendly, and open-minded at the same time: the best kind of teacher.

"Would anyone like to say anything at this time?" she says once we've all settled down. I raise my hand again.

"Adelaide, take it away," she says.

"Do you mind if I stand at the front of the class?" I say.

"No problem," she says.

I get up, the reverberation of my feet hitting the floor the only sound in the room other than bated breaths and fidgeting of other students.

"I'd like to direct this statement to the starter of this debate and his original question: Doesn't Eurymachus have a point? Tempting men by wearing tight-fitting clothes and putting on makeup, isn't that what women should avoid?" I look around the class with a fierce look in my eyes, daring someone to challenge me. "I would like to introduce to you an odd sort of specimen."

I walk to Mrs. Vaughn's desk, and I pick up the small pot sitting on her desk. "This"—I show it to everyone in the class—"is an Osiria rose."

Every student looks at it intensely, mystified. Nathaniel looks confused about how this monologue is making a point. I smirk and continue speaking. "An Osiria rose is usually red on the outsides and white on the inside."

I touch the red outer layer of one of the petals. "The red could represent a woman's physical appearance. She is delectable, the first thing that others see. It is beautiful and very appealing. After a couple of moments, you start to notice the white. It is also beautiful in its own way, although it is never as bold or as dominant as the red part."

The realization of what I'm going to say is starting to dawn upon the pupils of the class, and some people nod, encouraging me to go on.

"The Osiria rose is appreciated by people all over the world. Even people who don't really care about these kinds of things know the value of its beauty. Never would people pick apart this rose just for the pleasure of seeing it crumble. I wish that some people, regardless of gender, would acknowledge that. I wish that society would teach people 'don't rape' rather than 'don't get raped.' No matter how tempting Penelope was, I wish the suitors had the simple respect of a woman to cease bothering her when she clearly didn't want it. That is all."

I take the rose with me back to my seat, ignoring the stunned silence.

"Adelaide Lillvik-Trumbull, you are *something*." Troye sits down next to me at lunch, his tray of cafeteria food slamming onto the table with a loud clang.

"Osiria?" I ask. He nods. "All right."

"All right?" He is shocked at the normalcy of my answer. "*All right?*" He lowers his voice, eying the pot containing the rose, which is sitting on the table. "I know you drove home to go get it."

"How?" I inquire, not really that surprised.

"I saw it in your room last time I was there. And I have the same classes as you do. And none of the teachers have those kind of roses."

I raise my hands in defeat. "Okay, you got me."

He shrugs. "Not that hard to figure out."

We start discussing graduation and various pieces of classical music. "I can't believe you aren't valedictorian!" he exclaims. "Who knew the most wonderful Adelaide Lillvik-Trumbull, with all her philosophical conversations and tragic epiphanies, solver of the world's problems, couldn't be valedictorian?" He swoons dramatically, making him look silly.

"Oh, shut up," I say. "I don't really know Ivy Flores that well, but she seems nice enough. And her grades are impeccable. I'm not surprised."

He shifts in his seat. "I mean, I don't know anyone that well considering I've been here less than a year."

"I don't know," I say, nodding toward Zaidan and Arabella, who are sitting across from us, engrossed in their own discussion. "You seem to be doing okay with the three of us." I feign a serious expression. "That is, if we keep you."

He looks at me haughtily. "I assure you," he beams confidently. "I'll make it."

"Don't be so sure," I challenge.

"Guys . . . what's happening?" Zaidan asks curiously.

"Nothing." I shake my head. "What're you guys talking about?"

"The scope of the Full Faith and Credit Clause," Ara explains.

"Interesting."

Troye and I join in on the conversation eagerly, finding something complex and deeply opinionated to talk about exciting. Even though we all have similar mindsets, we still sound like we're arguing. It is peculiar. As I hear Zaidan's argumentative and authoritative tone, Ara's passionate rebuttals, and Troye playing the role of the devil's advocate, I realize that I am lucky to have them. I'm happy. Here are some words of wisdom: the only thing better than being long-lastingly happy is the realization that you are significantly happy. That is, until in your euphoric daze you realize that you will never be this happy for a long period of time, and that somewhere, sometime in your path toward inevitable death, there will be a roadblock of melancholy that bursts your bubble.

But I don't like thinking about that.

We start new pieces in orchestra for our spring concert. The whole group is energized, though that doesn't help because reading a piece for the first time will never sound good. At the end of the practice, Xavier can't resist talking to me about the earlier incident.

"I heard about what you did in Literature," Xavier says, grinning. "Nice job."

"Thanks," I say as I walk out the door.

I drop off Troye at his house. It has become a routine to save him from riding home on the bus as the sole senior. He is waiting by my car, as usual. This time, there is an anomaly. My car keys are twirling in his hands, jingling with the constant movement.

He smiles sheepishly. "Nicked them from you in orchestra."

I roll my eyes. "Doesn't matter if you have the keys; you still can't drive."

He frowns. It's a sore subject for him. "Thanks for bringing it up," he says sarcastically.

He is about to toss them to me when I say, "Keep the keys." He looks confused. "You can drive home today," I clarify.

He grins. "Thanks." He slides into the driver's seat excitedly, almost shaking. I roll my eyes again.

He drives faster than I do, and more erratically. I have noticed this before, and it is one of the reasons that I am hesitant to let him drive. Almost every twist and turn of the car is unexpected. If there is one thing I know about myself, it's that I don't like the unexpected. But I find myself enjoying the ride home for some reason, even though the wind whistles in my ears through the open windows and I start to develop a headache. Maybe I don't know myself as well as I think I do.

I don't know what I want to be when I grow up. Or, to put it in better terms, what I'm going to do when I graduate. Troye knows what he wants to do: he wants to be a physician. He hates hospitals, so it doesn't make sense to me. When I had brought this point forward, he shrugged his shoulders.

"I just like helping people," he'd say, then change the subject.

But I have no clue what I want to do—a testimony of how little I know myself.

He comes to a screeching halt in my driveway. He hands me the keys, bids me goodbye, and walks to his house. I can see him wringing his hands. He has picked up that habit from me, I know.

I sit in the car for a few minutes after I get a phone call, wringing my hands subconsciously and thinking of how to spend the rest of my evening. On a rare occasion, I have no homework. I haven't had free time in such a long time that it is an unnatural feeling. Remembering the look on Ara's face this morning, I decide to pay her a visit.

The drive there takes longer than usual because of the flood of tired students driving home from schools and the influx of exhausted employees. By the time I reach her home, the sun is barely touching the horizon, still providing feeble light. The lights aren't on in the house, but Ara's car is parked outside. I take the Osiria rose with me, hoping to give it to her as a peace offering.

Logan is not home yet, I can tell, because I don't hear chiming piano keys. Ara is the one who opens the door. She nods at me, and then gestures for me to come inside. We walk up the stairs, the rhythmic thuds the only sound in the room.

I take a seat on her bed when she first speaks, her voice rugged.

"Thanks for the rose," she says. "It's beautiful."

"No problem," I say awkwardly.

"You want to know what happened because of this morning." It is not a question. I am glad that it isn't.

I nod. "I just want to help."

She shakes her head. "You can't. I guarantee it." She shifts, now sitting cross-legged. I laugh, albeit not amused at all.

"You have no idea what I can and can't do. You'll never know that I can't help you if you never let me help in the first place."

She shrugs her shoulders, obviously considering it. After a moment of internal conflict, she seems to concede. "All right," she says. "Give it a go."

"First, you've got to tell me what happened."

"Um," she says. "So basically . . ." She recollects the events of what happened last night to me.

"Whoa," I say. "That's a whole lot of shit." I realize that I may have been pretty tactless, so I say sorry immediately afterward. She laughs heartily, and it's a relief to hear after such a long time. It's a genuine laugh. But her expression becomes somber after just a second, reminding both of us what we were talking about in the first place.

"Ara . . ." I say empathetically. "Here." I scoot forward. "Look at this." I roll up my sleeves. Her eyes widen in prospective horror. Instead of finding darkened scars, she finds faded writing. She grabs my arm and reads it, tracing the letters with her fingers.

"These say . . . *horrible things*," she barely whispers.

I smile at her confusion, knowing that she will understand in a moment. "These are things that people have said to me."

Ara looks shocked and in disbelief. "Would people really say these sorts of things to you?" She puts a hand over her mouth. "This is horrible."

"Yeah," I chuckle harshly. "I mean, at first, I was really affected by someone calling me a—*what did he call me again?*" I look at one of the more legible phrases written on my arm. "Oh, right. A *crazy, annoying, manipulative bitch*. But then . . ." I shrug my shoulders. "I realized that I don't care about what people that horrible and vile have to say about me."

"Then why do you have that shit written on your arm?" she inquires suspiciously. I smile again, throwing off her train of thought once more.

"When people say particularly hurtful things to me, I go home, grab a pen, and write what they said to me on my arm. Then, a couple of minutes later, or when I have a chance to, I wash it off with a good scrub with water and soap. It really does help."

"Well, the words haven't faded completely," she points out. "This is completely readable."

"Words take a great deal of time to fully heal."

She rolls her eyes. "Don't be a smartass."

"At least I'm smart," I reply. "You're just an ass."

She puts a hand over her heart. "Offended," she says plainly. Her expression changes as she thinks of something different.

"Adelaide . . ." She looks me in the eye. "Who was the one that said those things?"

I fidget. "My ex-boyfriend."

She looks incredulous. "You had a boyfriend? When? *Who?*"

I want to yell that I plead the fifth, but I know that Arabella deserves an answer.

"It was from winter of sophomore year to"—I squint my eyes—"I think the middle of June?"

She looks interested, but also a bit befuddled and infuriated. "Who was it though?"

"Do you remember Nathaniel Beauregard?"

She does a double take. "Nate? That's Zaidan's debate partner."

"Really?" I'm startled and slightly uncomfortable with this information. "I didn't think he could do anything but lie around and do nothing."

Ara shakes her head. "No, they've been debate partners since seventh grade. I'm surprised Zaidan didn't know that you dated him. They spend like three days a week together after school to review debate stuff . . ."

When I don't respond or react, there is an awkward silence.

"If you don't mind me asking," Ara says carefully. "Why did you break up?"

I think about it for the first time in months. "He cheated on me."

"That bastard!" Ara is furious. "I'm going to tell Zaidan to stop debating with him."

"Absolutely not!" I protest. "Don't do anything stupid."

She crosses her arms defiantly. "Why the hell shouldn't I? He should get retribution for being an absolute—"

"Ara!" I plead. "Can we *please* change the subject?"

She looks at me with a softened expression. Then, she sighs. "Fine," she says, "but one last question."

This time, I am the one to fold my arms. "One, and one only," I state firmly. "And I won't answer it if I don't feel comfortable answering it. No arguments."

"Oh, absolutely," she concedes, tapping her right foot impatiently.

I let out a resigned sigh and lean onto the wall. "Ask away."

She beams just before proceeding to ask her question. "How did nobody know that you were dating? I mean, you were in a relationship with one of the most blunt and forthright guys in the entire school for about half a year."

"We just didn't want people to make a big deal out of it." I laugh. "Looking back on it, he probably just suggested it because he didn't want to sleep with girls who knew he had a girlfriend. It probably would've made them a bit more reluctant."

She puts a hand on my arm. "Sorry, Adelaide."

"Even my mom didn't know," I add. I cover my face with my hands. "I was such an idiot."

"Wait," she says after a few moments. "Does Troye know?"

I shake my head. Then, she comes up with another question.

"Why do you have what Nathaniel said to you on your arm if you broke up over the summer?"

"Oh," I say, tracing my arm subconsciously. "That was only today."

"How?" she asks.

"I thought you said only one question," I state blandly.

She raises her hands in surrender. "Okay," she says apologetically.

"No; it's fine, I'll answer it anyway," I say quickly. "After the whole rose thing, he cornered me during a free period. Said he was sorry and that he wanted me back."

"What did you do?" she asks.

"Oh, I rejected him, of course." Ara looks pleased with my answer. "Then after I turned him down, he called me a bitch. It's why you can still read it, because I haven't gotten the chance to wash it off."

She stands up. "Come on," she says. "You're doing it now."

I walk into the bathroom and catch a glimpse of the trash basket. I see a discarded razor, its edge stained a dull brown. I look at Ara, trying to explain the concern and worry running through my head in a physical expression. She makes direct and intense eye contact with me, her chin up and an aura of defiance surrounding her.

"I'm never doing that shit again," she announces. "There's too much stuff to do and too many idiots to slap before I go out."

I smile at her. "That's the spirit," I say. I know she's probably saying this as a spur-of-the-moment sort of thing, but I do hope she sticks with it.

While I scrub my arm with fresh, floral-smelling soap, Ara asks me another question.

"Did you ever get revenge?"

"Not at the time of the breakup, no."

"Why not?" she complains.

"It wasn't worth my time," I explain. "Why mope over him when I could just move on with my life?"

"That's pathetic," she says, picking at her cuticles. "You should've done something."

"If it makes you feel better," I smirk, "I recorded our conversation at school, including the part when he called me a bitch, and sent it to Mrs. Beauregard. And his current girlfriend."

Ara looks at me with a peculiar expression for a couple of seconds. "I will never cross you, Adelaide Lillvik-Trumbull."

We've worked hard this year, the four of us. We skipped several lunches to study for tests, held study sessions every week at quiet bookstores. We have worked our asses off. After another one of these study sessions, held dangerously close to our finals, Troye and I linger in the bookstore for a bit longer than usual. My fingers trace over the spine of *War and Peace* by Leo Tolstoy, my favorite author.

"Have you ever read *War and Peace*?" Troye asks, eyeing the book.

I shake my head. "Surprisingly, no."

He looks at me in disbelief. "I thought you loved Tolstoy!"

"I do," I defend myself. "I've read pretty much everything but *War and Peace*."

He grabs a copy from the shelf and looks at the back. "Even *I* have read *War and Peace*."

"You have?" I am surprised. Troye has never struck me as the reading type.

"Twice," he says, sounding slightly offended. "It took me an extra read to understand it properly."

I nod vaguely.

He tucks the book under his arm. "I'm going to buy you this book," Troye announces.

I look at him oddly, not really processing what he has just said.

"Come on," he says, leading me to the checkout counter. "You're going to read *War and Peace*."

Right before we reach the front, I finally understand what exactly he's doing.

"No, no, no . . ." I say. "Don't waste your money on me."

He looks at me peculiarly. "You bought me a coffee the first day of school. Let me buy you a book."

"Absolutely not," I say firmly.

"Fine," he says defiantly. "I'll buy it for myself." He walks confidently to checkout. I cross my arms and follow him.

The next Monday, I find a badly gift-wrapped book sitting in my locker. There's a sticky-note attached to it, words written in Troye's tiny scrawl.

Don't return it (or try to) or you'll get another book and have me standing by your locker with a cup of coffee for you in my hand.

I shake my head and chuckle, which causes some people nearby to give me an odd look.

"Like my gift?" I hear Troye's voice behind me.

"Listen Troye, I can't—" I turn around and my words stop as my lips form a grin. There Troye is, hair damp from the warm drizzle of rain outside, holding a cup of coffee.

"Damn you!" I say. "You knew I was going to try and give it back to you."

He smiles and gives the coffee cup a small shake. "Be prepared, people always say."

I take the cup from him. His hands are cold. I put the cup right back in his hand. When I see his look of confusion, I explain. "You need it; you're freezing." He grabs the cup, shivering. "You need to drink all of that and take your jacket off."

I grab his free hand and pull him toward the front of the building. The cold feeling from his hand seeps into mine and I ignore it. "We're going to the orchestra room."

He follows me obediently. I wave to Xavier, who is strolling leisurely in the hallways. He looks at us holding hands and raises his eyebrows. I shake my head and roll my eyes.

"Did you walk here, Troye?" I ask when we are inside the warm embrace of the orchestra room. This is another reason I enjoy it in here: it's one of the warmest rooms in the school.

"Maybe."

"Oh, you idiot," I mutter under my breath while he sets his jacket on a chair, droplets of water still visible on the fabric. He shivers again.

I lead him to the closet, which has both of its doors closed. The vents are audible in the pin-drop silence, blasting out heat at a rapid pace.

"Because we don't have a blanket to warm you up, you're just going to have to use an empty bass bag." I hand him the black soft case.

"Really?" He raises his eyebrows, obviously skeptical.

"Just do it and don't complain," I say.

He is about to reply, probably with a witty remark, when he sneezes. It sounds delicate, like a kitten's sneeze. Then, when he finally makes sheepish eye contact with me, I give him an I-told-you-so look.

"I'll sit in the stupid bass case," he says under his breath.

"Good." I smile almost disgustingly sweetly.

He sits down and wraps himself in the soft bag, sipping coffee absentmindedly. I sit next to him, tapping my feet on the floor in a random pattern.

"There's still half left." Troye holds the cup in front of me, tempting me. "You can have it. It was for you, after all."

Reluctantly, I take the coffee from him. I don't regret it soon afterward when I feel much more awake because of the caffeine. "Thanks," I whisper.

The day drags on as I ignore everything else and read some Tolstoy. His writing is intriguing but dense, and overwhelming at times. Even Xavier seems distracted. He gives us a study hall today, giving me more time to read.

"Excellent book choice," he murmurs when he sees the colossal book lying across my lap.

I give him a nod in acknowledgment of his statement.

He asks if he can read the book after I finish it. "Haven't read it in a while," he says.

I smile. "Sorry Xavier, but you'd have to ask Troye. It's his copy, not mine."

He turns to the viola section eagerly, but finds that the boy who sits in first chair is missing. He looks at me for an answer.

"Dentist's appointment," I state.

"Unfortunate," he notes. "Would you like to stay and practice?"

"Sure," I say, right as the bell rings and everyone leaves the room.

The silence grows louder within seconds until I shatter it with a black violin and a bow. Xavier has gone to make copies of sheet music. I know I will be kicked out of the room soon. Rookwood is hosting an elementary school concert tonight, and they are using our room for warm-ups in an hour or so.

I hear the back door open and close when I am in the middle of practicing a piece. I assume it's one of the elementary kids, so, still playing, I speak. "I'll be gone in a minute!"

"Well, that's unfortunate because we were hoping to practice the pieces for our concert next week."

Idella and Prakash both smirk at me, making me twice as irritated.

"Oh." I rub on one of my sore shoulders. "It's just you two."

"Just us?" Prakash repeats. "Okay then."

Idella looks around the empty room. "Where's Troye?" she asks with her feathery voice. It is sometimes hard to remember that she plays bass. She grabs an instrument from an assortment of them on a rack against a wall. Prakash has wheeled in his own cello, the bright blue of the hard case distinctly visible.

Idella props herself on a bass stool, bow in hand. Prakash, his cello now out and properly tuned, begins to ruffle through sheet music.

"We only have about an hour," I say. "Then we've got to clear the room for the kids playing at the concert tonight."

Prakash nods his head in understanding, his eyes already scouring the first piece. Idella is applying rosin to her bow. We play for half an hour, altering pieces whenever we feel like it.

When Xavier comes back, he tells us to exit the premises in a formal and elegant fashion: he barges in and slumps down on a chair, papers set beside him in a stack on the floor. "I'm tired; get out," he says.

"Okay, okay," I say, packing my violin. "Give us a minute."

I am walking to the back of the school, headed toward my car, when I first hear it.

It is most definitely Zaidan's voice, but I have never heard it so angry before.

"We're debating this last tournament this year and then you and I are finding new partners."

He is standing at the entrance of an ostensibly empty classroom, his arms folded, his voice cold, his back straight, and his head held up high.

"You can't do that!" I hear frustrated pleas from another boy in the room, a voice very familiar to me: Nathaniel. "We've worked so hard on this, ever since the seventh grade!"

"That was before you called one of my best friends a bitch!" Zaidan is spitting venom. I decide that it's my time to leave. It would be insurmountably awkward if either one of them saw me right now. However, my feet are glued to the floor in a most uncomfortable fashion. I can't help but listen further.

"You don't know what she did to me!" Nathaniel practically bellows. "She deserved it!"

"Oh, of course," Zaidan's voice has acquired a sarcastic undertone. "She was the one that was caught screwing one of your friends. Sure."

"I apologized," Nathaniel tries to get Zaidan to see things from his perspective. "And—"

"She still wouldn't take you back?" I am worried about Zaidan's new tone with him. It is now soft and almost sympathetic. For the first time, I think, what if Zaidan takes Nathaniel's side? I know Ara never would; she was about to rip his head off last night. But what about Troye? Could I imagine him being the one glaring at me? Could I really handle another adversary?

Zaidan's voice jolts me back into reality. His voice has maintained its polite, airbrushed quality.

"I'm guessing that you asked her out again, and she rejected you."

"Yeah," Nathaniel sounds relieved. "You finally understand."

"Okay." Zaidan's tone has returned to a disapproving, grating sound, making my jaw clench. Zaidan is pensive, and I recognize the oncoming storm one second before it hits. Zaidan hits Nathaniel with every word, taking advantage of Nathaniel's numbing shock.

"You—absolute—bastard—" Zaidan has now grabbed the nearest book to him, and unfortunately for Nathaniel, it's an encyclopedia. Zaidan's arms are visibly struggling from the weight of the book, but that certainly doesn't stop him from hitting the other boy three times before setting the book down from mild exhaustion. While Nathaniel grips his arms, which are guaranteed to bruise tomorrow, Zaidan resumes his monologue.

"You have no right to expect a woman to date you at your beck and call." Zaidan laughs in disbelief, like he's laughing at an inside joke that only he knows. "I can't believe Adelaide tolerated you for more than thirty seconds. I mean, she can't even see your fucking head it's stuck so far up your own ass!" Nathaniel opens his mouth to respond, but stays silent. "Do you even know what Adelaide is like?" Zaidan is practically smiling. "She doesn't take any of that misogynistic shit. I can't believe you knew her for that long without figuring it out."

He starts to pack his bag and I realize that I need to evacuate the premises before things get awkward. My footsteps are suddenly ten times louder as I fly down the stairs. I almost don't notice that Troye has texted me.

Can you meet me at Barakah's? You know, if it's convenient. He is always so formal when it comes to texting that it makes me laugh from the sheer awkwardness of it.

Ok, I text back. *Give me ten minutes.*

As my phone shuts off with an almost inaudible click, I drive onto the main road off campus. It is good timing, I note, because I can see a horrendously bright-yellow school bus pass me as I wait at an intersection. *Cherokee Elementary School,* it proclaims in bold black letters. I see unfamiliar faces staring back at me. That is, until the end of the bus. I see Tai, clutching a bass with one arm. She smiles and gives me a wave. I return the gesture. Then the bus passes and the red light changes to green, and I am flung once more into my journey to Barakah's. I wonder why he has made sure that I come to the café this time. We usually meet there at least twice a week for studying. When I get there, I realize that much like this morning, Troye has walked to Barakah's from his home because his floppy hair is soaking wet. He is practically asking to get sick.

"Hi," he says with a sniffle, offering me a coffee. I take it.

"What's wrong?" I say. I can tell that there is something wrong just by the look on his face.

He looks surprised that I know that there is an anomaly in his behavior. "Oh, nothing's wrong," he assures me. "I just wanted to tell you something."

I sit down, my book bag landing on the floor with a loud thud. I interlace my fingers and set my elbows on the table. "Tell me," I state.

He speaks with no hesitation, no suspense, and direct eye contact. "I applied to Emory for my medical career."

I grin in relief. I thought his news was going to be much worse. "That's fantastic!" I say. "I'm really proud of you."

"Thanks," he tries to say nonchalantly, although the excitement in his eyes seeps into his voice.

"And speaking of colleges," I say. "I've got to tell you something as well."

"Go ahead," he says understandingly.

"I've applied to Georgia Tech. I want to be an engineer." I squint my eyes pensively. "Or, at least, it's the most compatible career choice for me." I shrug my shoulders and grip the sides of my chair with my hands. "In all honesty, I don't really know what exactly I want to be."

Troye smiles. "At least you're trying. College will help you figure it out, I guess."

I set my mug down and lean back in my seat. "I can't believe it," I say. "We're going to *college.*"

He chuckles and runs a hand through his hair. "I can hardly believe it too. We're actually growing up. We're all going to live our own separate lives."

"The two of us are going to be stuck together for a bit longer," I point out. "We're potentially going to be in the same state."

He chuckles again. "Indeed, we are."

We watch the newly made raindrops race down the large window by our table. "I'm calling Ara and Zaidan," Troye says. "It's an impromptu study session."

I find this arrangement to be very agreeable, and I voice my opinion to Troye. While he phones Zaidan, I ask, "Should I call Ara?"

He shakes his head and checks his watch. "Knowing them, by this time they're probably in the same place."

I nod, even though I know that is not a guaranteed possibility because I saw Zaidan alone a few minutes ago.

When he gets off the phone, he gives it a peculiar look. "Turns out that they're not together right now," he clarifies.

"I'll call Ara then," I reply. It takes three rings for her to pick up.

When I turn off my phone, I give the ever-expectant Troye the news. "Ara's coming too.

It'll take her a bit longer because she's at a park of some sort."

"Okay," Troye says. "I wonder what she's doing there."

I shrug my shoulders. "No clue."

After a moment of unequivocally awkward silence, I speak again. "Oh, you'll never guess who I saw today!"

"Who?" he inquires.

"Tai," I say brightly. "I think she's playing at Rookwood tonight with Cherokee's orchestra."

"We should go!" Troye is excited, and he is giving me a pleading look that seems to say *please* a million times.

"Okay," I concede. "But you're the one calling Zaidan and Ara. Tell them to come to Rookwood."

"Deal," he says. "What time does the concert start?"

"Seven," I say. "If we leave now, we can make it."

I grab my car keys when he gives me another pleading look. "No, Troye James Saavedra," I enunciate dramatically. "You cannot drive."

Being at school after hours, especially during concerts and/or other performances, gives me a sense of power and unexplainable tranquility. It is probably because of the lessened enforcement of rules that would be airtight during the school day. (It is more stressful, however, if you're sneaking into the grounds late at night on an excursion to the Tower.) I feel as if I can breathe easier. I will not be playing tonight, I remind myself.

Seeing the miniature instruments and the small children in tuxedos and dresses, I can't help but feel nostalgic for simpler times.

I notice that the kids aren't even worried about playing in front of such a large group. They couldn't care less. All they are occupied with at the moment is talking amongst each other about things that I don't have the faintest clue about.

Troye and I decide to wait out in the hall for the performance to begin and for the volunteers to let us in the auditorium.

I see Tai with two people I can assume to be her parents. Her dad is a frail-looking man who reacts to every single sound emitting from the noisy school. I wonder if he was always this way. He is carrying two cases: one holding a violin, and (I assume) the other containing a viola.

Her mother, on the other hand, is a statuesque woman who is slightly intimidating. She wears a deep-purple dress and dark makeup, which suit her. Her hair is in a tight and severe bun. She wheels a cello behind her, yet she still looks poised and elegant at the same time. I can see how Tai resembles her, a vivid, striking face and an air of sophistication present around both of them.

Tai sees Troye first, and her face lights up. She did seem to like him a lot better than me the last time we met, although Ming preferred me (possibly because of the ingenious technique of bribery by means of cookies).

"Hi!" she squeals, running up and giving him a big hug. She is quite short for her age, and she only reaches his waist. Nevertheless, this doesn't deter her. She sees me next, giving me a similar (albeit less tight) hug.

"What're you doing here?" she asks. "I thought you went home, Adelaide."

"Troye and I came back to see you guys play," I explain.

"Hello," a smooth voice says. Tai's mom holds her hand out for me to shake it. "It is nice to meet you. I am Tai's mother."

"Nice to meet you." I give her a smile, which she returns cautiously. The same process occurs with Troye. Then, she steps back to her husband (who has made no effort for social interaction) and lets Tai do the talking.

"I'm going to be playing a different instrument for every song!" Tai says excitedly. "First I'm going to play in the first violin section, then cello, then viola, then bass."

"That's really cool," I say, trying to make my voice as pleasant as I can. For some reason, I really want this girl to like me.

"We can't wait to hear you play," Troye adds enthusiastically.

"Thank you." Tai blushes.

"Tai, dear . . ." Her father speaks for the first time. His voice is as fragile as glass, and he behaves like every sound around him is a hammer waiting to shatter his speech. "Ming is waiting outside the theater. We have to put your instruments inside the room and go to her."

His English, no matter how fluent or eloquent it may actually be, will always sound strained if he continues to speak so quietly.

"Okay, Dad!" Tai chirps. She takes no notice of her father's odd behavior and skips into the orchestra room, which is a difficult feat considering she is carrying a bass. I wince when the scroll hits the side of the door. Her mother laughs, almost forcefully, and she grabs the door with her free hand and pulls it wide open so Tai and the bass can pass through unharmed. Tai's dad follows his family into the room of nervously ecstatic children.

Troye checks his phone absentmindedly. Without looking up, he says, "Ara and Zaidan are already seated. They said to hurry up, we might not even get a proper spot at this rate."

He does not see me grinning at him amusedly until he looks up. "What?" he says. When I don't answer, he repeats the question. Then, he instinctively flattens his hair.

I shake my head, trying to keep myself from laughing. "I think Tai has a tiny crush on you," I clarify.

He looks at me with an expression of utmost confusion. "What?"

I laugh heartily, unable to withhold it anymore. "Did you see her? She blushed every single time you spoke to her."

"That's not—" Troye is cut off by the opening of the door once more. He turns around, severely irritated, but then his expression softens as he realizes that it is Tai's parents. I try not to laugh, and he tries not to turn red. When they finally turn the corner of the hall, we both fail at our set tasks.

I flutter my eyelashes dramatically. "Hi Troye," I say in an overly girly voice.

"Shut up," he mutters. "This is way too awkward."

"All right, all right," I say, giving him a break.

We walk to the theater looking distinctly different compared to the folks that have shown up. The rest are older, parents of children that are playing. They are all formally dressed. That streak breaks when we show up; Troye is wearing his usual jeans/plaid combination while I am wearing jeans and an oversized red sweater. Indeed, we are the epitome of formal.

As soon as I see the rows of seats filled up, I know we won't be able to find seats next to each other. I tell Troye to follow me and we go to the one place I know we will get a decent view.

"Exactly *what* are you doing in the control booth?" the boy operating the booth hisses. "The show's about to start any minute now!"

"Hi, Easton," I say, exasperated. "I know there's a performance; that's why Troye and I are here."

He looks at me like I am insane.

I grab a stool from the back of the room and set it in front of the large window facing the stage. "Do you mind if we watch the performance from in here?"

Easton considers it. He stares out into the large audience, probably looking for a couple of adjacent, empty seats to alleviate himself of the burden of having two extra people in the room. Finding none, he looks at the technological equipment adoringly before speaking resignedly. "Here are the rules: no speaking, no moving, no touching any of my equipment, and," he looks at us oddly, "no physical contact. The last thing I need is for Principal Pomeroy to walk in here with you two making out."

I chuckle awkwardly. "Deal."

"And we're not dating, so that won't be a problem," Troye adds quickly.

"Perfect," Easton says, slightly relieved. "Now sit down, stay out of my way, and shut up."

"Sounds like a plan," I say jovially (perhaps overly so, because Easton gives me a withering look).

We sit down and lean against the back wall as soon as the lights are dimming. Easton gives us a final warning to remain silent by dramatically turning around and putting a finger over his lips, his hazel eyes wide and menacing. Then he turns on a microphone of some sort. When he speaks, his voice reverberates around the room and the auditorium as well.

"Ladies and gentlemen, Rookwood High School is proud to host the Cherokee Elementary School Orchestra!" There is polite applause, followed by some overenthusiastic cheers from the parents sitting in the first few center rows. They all, no matter what race, look strangely alike, holding up different sorts of cameras and cell phones to record what their children, years from now, will cringe at.

The concert begins. I would love to say that they sound perfect, and that the quality of the music exceeds my expectations. However, I must say very truthfully: they sound bad. There is bad posture and pitchy notes and wrong speeds.

However, the kids on stage don't seem to care at all. They seem happy enough just playing in front of people, or rather, just playing at all. It doesn't matter if they get notes wrong or don't sit on the edge of their chairs; *they are happy*. Throughout the performance, I can see Tai switch from instrument to instrument and section to section without any major mishaps. I can see toothless smiles and bright eyes and pure passion. I revere them for being so content with themselves, and I wish I could do the same.

I remember a quote from one of my favorite composers, Gabriel Fauré. He once said, "I played atrociously . . . no method at all, quite without technique, but I do remember that I was happy; and if that is what it means to have a vocation, then it is a very pleasant thing." Perhaps there are future Faurés in this very theater.

When it is over, I get up and stretch. Troye does the same, his hands easily reaching the low ceiling.

Troye and I thank Easton, and then we set off to find Zaidan and Ara.

They are sitting on a bench outside the orchestra room, one that Troye and I had neglected to use while waiting in the same hall before the concert.

Zaidan looks up first. "I knew you guys would show up somewhere around here," he says.

"Interesting concert, wasn't it?" Ara says, a smirk playing on her lips.

"Yeah, I especially liked when Troye's admirer kept switching sections," I joke.

"Oh, but you weren't playing this concert, were you?" Troye inquires innocently. "I didn't know you could switch sections."

Evidently, my joke has backfired, and Zaidan and Ara find it hilarious. Even I can't help but to crack a smile after a few moments. Nevertheless, I must respond.

"Shut it, Washingturd," I quip.

Ara is almost brought to tears by laughter and has to be carried out by a still-chuckling Zaidan.

Troye

I HAVE NEVER FELT MORE UNCOMFORTABLE, ANXIOUS, AND excited in my entire life. I am graduating. It is a peculiar and unnatural feeling to think that I am actually growing up. Yet the exhilarating thought of being independent and learning how to make my way in the world makes the snakes in my stomach writhe with both anticipation and loathing. But I am actually doing it: I will be flung into the real world in a matter of hours.

It does scare me. I mean, it should. But honestly, it doesn't. I am ready to study more about what actually interests me, and I am ready to launch my medical career—or at least, this is as ready as I'll ever be.

The program is surprisingly short, with a speech from Pomeroy, another from one keynote speaker, a small speech by the valedictorian, Ivy Flores, and the handing over of high school diplomas. But before all of this happens, there is one event that is the most important to me: Adelaide and I are playing "Enigma," which I am terrified about. Xavier has been texting us words of encouragement all day. However, I haven't seen him since I've been here, and I'm starting to panic.

Right at the last moment, mere minutes before I get on stage and lose all hope of Xavier showing up, the happiness deflating inside me, I receive another text from him. *I can't come. Aaliyah is sick.*

I type back hurriedly, not caring if I have made stupid punctuation and grammatical errors.

Sorry about that but who exactly is she? Adelaide won't tell me.

I get the response almost immediately.

Aaliyah is my daughter. She's four, and she's adopted. Not that that actually matters at all.

Oh . . . I say. That clarifies a lot. Thanks.

No problem, he replies. *Listen, I've got to go. She's puking again. Good luck.*

Thanks. I hope Aaliyah feels better.

There is no response, but I don't anticipate one arriving any time soon.

Suddenly, there is a heavy hand on my shoulder. Principal Pomeroy gives me a reassuring smile. "You'll do great," he says.

"Thank you." I surprisingly feel significantly better. If a man like Pomeroy, who barely knows me, can have so much faith in me as to let me play at my own graduation, then there is no way I'm going to let him down.

I find Adelaide quickly. Rather than wearing her graduation gown, she is wearing a black dress that ends right below her knees. She has her violin and bow in one hand, and sheet music in another.

"Let's do this," she says, striding past me. I wish I could feel as confident as she sounds.

When we get up there, I realize a vital piece of information: if I mess up, no one but Adelaide will know that I have messed up. This makes me feel invigorated. I hear a few cheers from who I assume to be Ara and Zaidan, but I tune it out. All I need to do to get through this is focus on the music. In the end, it isn't about my skill level, or how long I have been playing the viola. It's about me being confident with myself as a player. I just have to convince myself into thinking that, and that's all it takes.

The viola seems tiny and breakable for the first time since I held it for the first time. My fingers seem too big and clumsy, and I can feel my palms sweating under the neck of the instrument. The first notes are shaky, and I panic as I struggle to remember the notes. Eventually, I start becoming more comfortable, envisioning me alone in my room. The notes, bless Xavier, are long and graceful, allowing for some error before smoothly transitioning into them. I try and focus on my breathing, and thankfully, it is over before I know it.

The applause lasts a lot longer than I thought it would, and Adelaide and I take deep bows. It is over. Now all I must do is sit back in my assigned chair and relax. My heart is still beating rapidly, as if I'm about to be called up to the stage to play once more. I know that I am done, but I can't seem to convince myself of that fact.

I barely understand any of what the next speaker says. He is impossibly old and has a frail yet deep voice, which is an unsavory combination.

Next up is Ivy Flores. She is very short, and neither thin nor large. She has dark-brown skin and a head full of frizzy, black hair. Her black eyes are bright with unexplainable emotion. I have never personally met her, so I pay attention to this speech. I want to know why she is valedictorian. She hesitantly taps the microphone that is fixed on the podium. After finalizing that it is indeed on, she begins her speech.

Her voice is shaky at first, growing confidence as she gets comfortable with so many people looking at her at once. "Hello," she says. "My name is Ivy Flores, and most of you probably don't know me." There are a couple of halfhearted chuckles before she resumes her speech.

"I would like everyone to take one single minute from the very important, honorable task of updating Instagram or Twitter, or ignoring the bumbling idiot standing in front of you that somehow managed to become valedictorian." She gestures to herself vaguely, and, surprisingly, a lot of students put their phones down.

"Take one minute to think about what your answer was every single time in your life someone asked you what you wanted to be when you grew up. Would it be a movie star, a singer, a doctor, or a vet? What did you say? Did it ever change throughout the years? Did the future ice skater turn into the ambitious doctor? Did the impassioned doctor eventually become the aspiring scientist in the field of complex rheology and biomechanics?"

People nod in assent, and there is a hushed aura that hangs over the crowd. Ivy smiles confidently, now standing up taller and with her head held a fraction of an inch higher.

"As a child, all of these jobs had no significance to me. I was more interested in something else: the occupation of saving the world. It didn't seem like a big ordeal to me.

"Why not save the world instead of, I don't know, manufacture toothpaste tubes? I had to do something—to rise above the injustice of squeezing toothpaste out of a tube when on the other side of the world, a child squeezes his mother's hand, finally finding food after days of starvation. As I grew older, however, I realized that I couldn't do it all, and that was the most difficult thing to accept about myself."

I can see now why she was chosen.

"As even more years passed by, I understood that it was okay. Do me one favor. Tell yourself that it is okay. It's okay to be a happy toothpaste-tube manufacturer versus being a lawyer that wallows in depression.

"And you don't have to be a lawyer or a toothpaste-tube maker—it doesn't matter. That is the beauty of this situation. Even though we've graduated and finally made it over this treacherous mountain of an achievement, we don't have to change ourselves immediately and adapt to the high standards of being a self-supporting adult. Take a second to revel in the fact that we have time to get used to the unfamiliar madness. I need you to do this for me, to see that you are a completely unprecedented person.

"The next part of this speech is about character. You were expecting it, weren't you? Let's be honest—I have to follow the generous, sometimes irritating precedence of those before me. High school is only a small part of the honorable quest to find ourselves. It allows us to understand who we are, and what we truly enjoy. This time is completely experimental, and we will make mistakes, and expose our own flaws, but that is what make us human. Trial and error shapes our skin."

She looks at the crowd with a fierce look in her eyes that reminds me much of Adelaide.

"We ourselves are the ones to decide whether to be shaped as a toothpaste tube maker, a lawyer, or neither. And this time, there is no one to tell us whether we are right or wrong."

She steps off the stage to endless roaring applause, and I don't think I've ever been so impressed with someone in my entire life. I look next to me, and I can see Adelaide crying and smiling at the same time. She wipes her eyes when she thinks no one is looking.

I learn something tantalizingly true in that moment. Happiness is not an inherent state. It is up and down, a veritable fluctuation. When it is present, a person must treasure it, though it may fade away.

I can see the brightness in Adelaide's eyes, shining out from behind her tears of joy. She is happy, and that is something that I value greatly. After a few moments of chatter, the entire graduation ceremony begins.

It's simple; we are herded by last name into alphabetically accurate lines, Pomeroy mispronounces some of the names of the ex-students, and then it's over.

After the ceremony ends, the crowd of graduates and family members moves into the blissfully air-conditioned building next to the outdoor site where we received our diplomas. Everyone is seated leisurely at scattered circular tables.

I sit down at a large table with Zaidan, Ara, Adelaide, Idella, Prakash, and a few other people. Out of the corner of my eye, I can see Zaidan's parents, my mom, Adelaide's mom, and, surprisingly, her father at a table. Mr. Trumbull is balding quickly, and he sits opposite Ms. Lillvik. The grandiose centerpieces prevent them from making uncomfortable eye contact. While the women at the table talk animatedly together, the men make small talk. I should not be bothered that my father is not here, but the thought lingers in the back of my head.

Rookwood has gone all out for this event. We have servers waiting on every table. We sit and relax while the servers bustle around us, dodging obstacles. A few times, Adelaide looks like she wants to stand up and help them. I resist the urge to laugh.

After we are done eating and most of the students have evacuated the hall, the four of us are perched on a minute hill outside. We can hear the loud chatter of the people standing outside of the glittering lights of the building. Darkness surrounds us with an eerie feeling. I am content. I'm well aware that my bubble of happiness will burst, but right now I am unaffected.

"Excuse me?" A waiter has ventured outside. He is looking at me directly.

"Yes," I say curiously.

He holds out a small, brown paper bag no bigger than my palm. "Someone told me to give this to you," he says.

"Which person?" I say while I accept the bag hesitantly.

He shrugs. "I have no clue."

He walks off back to the building before I can ask him any more questions.

"Should I open it?" I ask.

"Do it," Ara urges excitedly.

I do what I am told. Inside the bag, rather anticlimactically, is a key. I don't understand for a moment, but then I do. I have only recently obtained my driver's license. Before I can let out a high-pitched squeal like a child, I see a note folded in halves tumble out of the bag, almost going unnoticed.

Click the key to find out which one is yours, it reads. I walk toward the middle of the parking lot, and click the lock button hopefully. The small beep comes from the corner of the parking lot, and I follow the sound repeatedly until I see it.

It is a beautiful car, better than Adelaide's Mercedes. It is a dark-blue Jaguar XK Convertible, and I am instantly in love. I see a note taped to the steering wheel, but instead of opening the car, I run to find my mom.

She is outside the pavilion, discussing something with a woman that I don't recognize. I run up and give her a hug before she can react.

"Thank you so much," I repeat over and over in her ear.

She laughs heartily while pulling away from me. She looks at me with a befuddled expression, a smile still plastered on her face. "What're you thanking me for, dear?"

"For the gift you gave me," I answer her.

She looks genuinely confused now. "Sweetheart," she says. "I didn't even give you your present yet."

"What do you mean? Wasn't it you who gave me the . . ." My voice trails off.

"Troye, who gave you what?" She sounds concerned.

"Give me a minute," I say hurriedly, already breaking into a run toward the car. I unlock the door quickly and pull the door open. Inside, the note is waiting for me.

> Troye,
> I know that you're probably really confused right now, and I know why. I know you won't forgive me, and I've already accepted that. I wouldn't forgive my old man if he did something like that to me. This is my last gift to you, even though I know you probably wouldn't accept it if I was actually there. Have fun driving your girlfriend around.
> -Ivan

I read the note again and then rip it in half. In quarters. Eighths. I rip it over and over again until there are tiny slivers of paper. I stick the remnants of the note in my front pocket securely, where they are guaranteed not to fall out.

Explaining how I got a brand-new car to my mother is just as awkward as one would think. I wring my hands and hear the cracking of my knuckles. I wish Adelaide hadn't given me this habit.

"So . . ." my mom begins. "If I understood correctly, your dad just bought you a car. Just out of the blue."

I nod. "Pretty much."

She shrugs. "Okay. Fine with me."

"Really?" I say, shocked that she has taken the news so well. "That's actually all you're going to say?"

She raises her hands up. "What else am I supposed to do? Dance?"

"Sure, Mom," I say sarcastically.

She takes it literally. She starts to do a spasm of sorts, and I am completely embarrassed.

"Mom," I plead. "Please stop."

"Stop what?" she says, still flailing. I walk away swiftly.

"Bye, Mom," I yell back to her. She laughs loudly.

Adelaide is leaning against my new car. "Hi," she says. "I guess you get to drive me now."

I hold up the car key. "I guess so."

"Can you drop me home, then?" Adelaide asks. "Because I arrived in my mom's car. I don't really have a ride home."

"I have so much power now." I grin. "And of course I'll drop you home."

I sit in the driver's seat, breathing in the smell of leather. I plug my phone into an awaiting AUX cord. Adelaide grimaces at first. Her features soften when she realizes that she recognizes the piece and, big surprise: it has no words.

"'String Quartet in E Minor'?" Adelaide asks. "Fauré, right?"

"Yep," I respond. "Surprised?" She looks at me, confused. "You know, because my music choice is so horrible."

"It's getting better," she notes.

"I'm honored," I reply dryly.

When we get to our neighborhood, she says, "Pull into my driveway, not yours."

"Okay," I say, not bothering to ask why. After knowing Adelaide for this long, whenever she tells me to do something, I just go with it. She has a higher purpose, a philosophical plan for everything. I trust her to keep me unharmed.

"Come inside," she says cryptically, no emotion in her voice or on her face to give me some premonition of what's to come.

We enter her room and I sit on the edge of her bed, tapping my feet nervously. Her back is to me while she fishes something out of her closet.

"Don't be nervous," she states calmly. "It's nothing bad."

"Are you sure?" I am still tapping my feet.

She turns around, a small box in her hand, and plops down next to me. I didn't notice this morning that her nails are painted a deep royal purple.

"I can guarantee it," she assures.

"I'm trusting you, Adelaide," I say warningly.

"Like always," she responds.

Before I can retort, she hands me the box. It weighs almost nothing. "This is for you," she says, drumming her fingers on her legs.

"You didn't have to get—I didn't get you anything—"

"Shut up and open it." She is the one that sounds nervous now. "I hope you like it."

I uncover the box slowly, and I see two pieces of paper. "What's this—oh my *God*." I put a hand over my mouth. "You did *not*; oh my God, you *did*."

I hold the tickets to an Atlanta Symphony Orchestra performance in my hand. "Thank you so much. Oh my God; I love you so much. I really do. Thank you."

"It's really not a problem." Adelaide looks satisfied with herself. "And if you haven't noticed," she adds, "there's two tickets in the box. You get a plus-one."

She puts her hand on my shoulder and turns her head so her face is directly facing mine. "I want to let you know that you get to invite anyone, Troye, but if it isn't me, I will be deeply disappointed."

I chuckle. "So you buy me a coffee, I buy you a book, and in return, you buy me concert tickets?"

"Pretty much," Adelaide sighs. "But technically the last one's for myself too." She folds her arms. "That is, if I can be your plus-one."

"These are for next Saturday?" I inspect the tickets.

"Yeah." She is wringing her hands.

"Adelaide?" I look at her pensively.

"What?" She looks confused.

"Are you free next Saturday? There's an ASO performance and I'd absolutely love for you to come with me."

Adelaide smiles widely. "Sure." She stands up. "Do I have to drive you?" She smirks.

I shake my head while standing up. I can look more intimidating now, as I have to look down to see her. She has to look up to see my face, yet she still looks more intimidating than I do. But I guess that's just how Adelaide works. "I've actually got a car now," I say cheekily. "I think I can take you."

"Well that's good." She puts a hand on her hip. "See you Saturday, then."

She holds the bedroom open for me and gestures for me to exit the room. I step out into the hall. We walk down to the front door in silence.

"See you later then," I say.

"Bye." She is about to shut the door when I speak suddenly.

"Adelaide?" I say.

"Yeah?" She stares at me with wide eyes.

"Remember 'String Quartet in E Minor'?" I say, not exactly sure where I'm going when I'm saying this.

"Fauré, yeah?"

I nod.

"What about it?"

"Well." I dig my heels into the ground. "I've got the sheet music, and I was wondering if you want to play it? I can invite Prakash to play cello and Ana to play second violin."

She stares at me pensively. "Sure," she says after a moment. "Should I come over now?"

"Oh, no," I state hurriedly. "I've got . . . stuff to do."

"Oh," she says nonchalantly. "Okay."

I bid her goodbye.

Now all I need to do is find sheet music for that piece.

About two weeks later, on a warm summer's night, the four of us (christened with the most horrendous title, The Quirky Quartet, by Zaidan), are sitting lakeside on a thin blanket at about ten p.m. Lake Moore, about half an hour from my home, is a good place to think. Everyone deserves a good place to think. For me, it was a hidden room in my old home. It was dusty and it smelled like old shoes, but I liked having a place where no one could bother me.

I can tell that the lake is Adelaide's thinking place. She has a content smile plastered to her face, and her posture is a lot more relaxed. Instead of speaking to the rest of us, who are engaging in topic-less chatter, she is seated a couple of feet in front of us, knees tucked to her chest, gazing at the lake. She seems to be immersed in her own thoughts, not the view. It's an intriguing view, someone lost in her own personal odysseys.

After a few moments of listening in on Zaidan and Ara's conversation, I scoot forward.

Adelaide is evidently startled. "Did I interrupt anything?" I ask.

"No," she shrugs. "Maybe. But you can't really interrupt anything, can you? I'm here alone. Nothing to interrupt."

I fold my arms loosely. "You're finally wrong about something," I say audaciously.

"And why would that be?" Adelaide challenges.

"Because there *is* something to interrupt," I answer. "You and your thoughts can be considered two separate entities at the moment. You have reactions to your own thoughts, triggering several more."

"Good point," Adelaide notes.

"I'm getting better at this," I say. "You know, the whole 'philosophical genius' aspect of myself."

She laughs, a very crisp sound on this quiet night.

"Ivy's speech was awesome," I state, changing the subject. "It actually makes me think that everyone at Rookwood High School has to be philosophically competent before they get admitted to the school."

She nods her head, laughing again. "Yes, Troye. That's exactly how it works. You've figured it out. Rookwood has philosophically based admissions. It's not like it's a public school or anything."

I smile arrogantly. "Thanks."

"Hey, guys?" Zaidan calls out to us.

"What's up?" I turn around.

"So, I need to tell you something."

"Get on with it," Adelaide says gently.

"I'm moving to Chicago."

My first reaction is to look at Arabella, whose eyes are wide. I know that she is going to announce her decision tonight too.

"What for?" Adelaide asks. "And for how long?"

"How long, I can't answer," Zaidan says shakily. "I'm moving there because I got accepted to the Kendall College. It's a culinary school."

"That's excellent!" Adelaide says excitedly.

"While we're making grand announcements . . ." Ara starts hesitantly. She looks at me for affirmation to continue, and I nod encouragingly. "I applied to Emory at the same time as Troye." She looks at Zaidan almost guiltily. "And, like him, I got in."

She is expecting Zaidan to be upset, but that is exactly the opposite of what he's doing.

He leans over and gives her a hug and a kiss. "That's amazing!"

"You're not angry?" Ara asks.

"Of course not!" Zaidan clearly shows that he thinks the idea is blasphemous.

"You know how tough long-distance relationships—"

"I don't care," Zaidan blurts. "I really don't. Your job isn't to follow me around everywhere, Arabella." I am surprised that he uses her full name. "You have your own aspirations and dreams. I can't expect you to adapt to mine."

Ara looks like she's about to cry, and she looks down. "Thank you so much," she whispers. Zaidan puts a hand on her cheek. I almost want to look away from the simple intimacy of the action.

"Hey," he says softly. "You have nothing to thank me for."

"When are you leaving?" Ara asks hesitantly, hiccupping.

Zaidan is the one that looks down this time. "In one month. I have to get there a month earlier, you see."

Ara nods encouragingly and smiles, simultaneously sad and proud. "I guess I'll see you in a while, then."

"I guess you will," he replies. "But really," he adds urgently. "We can make this work. I know we can."

Ara laughs weakly. "Since when have I ever doubted your capabilities?"

Zaidan smiles lopsidedly. "Vice versa, sweetheart."

I didn't know if I believed in love, but these two guarantee its existence.

"What're you doing, Adelaide?" Zaidan asks.

"For college?" She wrings her hands. "I'm going to Georgia Tech in the fall. I was going to take a gap year, but I decided not to. It'd be too much time with nothing to do."

After fifteen minutes of talking and thinking, Ara starts distributing Tupperware boxes containing an assortment of food.

"Another announcement," Ara starts. Zaidan stops eating.

Ara looks at him, letting him finish the declaration. "We're taking a road trip," Zaidan says. "We've been planning it since the beginning of second semester."

"And you planned to tell us when?" Adelaide asks sarcastically, sitting with her legs crossed.

Zaidan beams at her grossly. "Right about now, sweetie," he drawls.

"All right. I'm in, only if you get that disgusting smile off your face this instant, Zaidan Markley," Adelaide offers.

"Fair enough."

"What about you, Troye? You in?" Ara asks.

"Where are we going?"

Zaidan and Ara look at each other nervously. "Florida, actually. If you don't mind."

They look at me anxiously. I don't want to disappoint them. "That's fine." I am pretty sure that the events that occurred in Florida will haunt me for the rest of my life. However, I also think that one day I'm going to have to face the ghosts that do the haunting. One day, I will have to face the sharp scent of whiskey, raised voices, and the color brown. It should be like ripping a Band-Aid off. The faster I do it, the more time I will have to recover.

"In fact," I add, "why don't I show you guys around my hometown?"

"Tampa, you mean? You really want to go there?" Ara's voice is delicate and concerned.

I justify my insanity. "I need to rip the Band-Aid off."

"Okay, if you really want to . . ." Zaidan shrugs his shoulders. "I'm cool with it."

Adelaide has not said a word since I suggested my idea. "What do you think?" I ask her.

She stares at me calculatingly before speaking. "Brave." She says no more.

"It's final!" Zaidan slices through the awkwardness. "We leave to Florida in a fortnight!"

In a whirlwind of immeasurably quick moments, the four of us are about to pile into Zaidan's hybrid, as it is the most cost efficient. It is eight a.m., and after a month of staying up late and waking up at eleven, I am tired.

"Shotgun," Ara says sleepily.

"Fine with me," I respond, half asleep. "Adelaide, be forewarned that I am stretching my legs in the back. I need my sleep."

She checks her watch. "It's 8:15!" she protests.

"Exactly," I say. "It's 8:15."

She crosses her arms, frustrated, although the tiniest of smiles throws away the idea of any seriousness.

"Don't tell me you've been getting up at school time, Adelaide," Zaidan adds to the conversation as he hoists his luggage into the car. He has the most out of all of us because as soon as we reach the end of our trip, he will be taking a flight from Tampa to Chicago. His parents will send the rest of his belongings at a later time.

"Is it really that horrible that I do?"

"Honestly, Del," Ara says in disbelief. "You are an utterly unprecedented teenager."

Adelaide grins, almost maniacally. "I know."

Zaidan plops down into the driver's seat. "Hey guys," he says. "Just a small surprise for you."

"And what is that?" Adelaide says suspiciously.

"Relax Adelaide; it's not bad," Zaidan says with a self-satisfied smirk. "We're going to go to the Georgia Aquarium today."

"Oh," Adelaide says. "Okay."

"I know what you're thinking," Zaidan says. "Well, all of us except you, Troye. With the exception of Troye, we've all been there tons of times." He starts absentmindedly tapping the steering wheel. "But this time shall be different!" he announces jovially. "They have a new exhibit up, and I think it's going to be good."

"Great," I say. "I haven't been there since I still lived in Florida."

"Why'd you come to the Georgia Aquarium of all places?"

"Orchestra trip. Our conductor was Georgian and held sentimental attachment."

"Simply fascinating," Zaidan states dryly, not taking his eyes off the road.

I stretch my legs and set them over Adelaide's, leaning my back on the locked car door. She gives me a dirty look, but she doesn't move.

"With traffic, we'll get there in about forty-five minutes," Ara notes after she checks the GPS on her phone.

"I'm going to take a nap," I announce.

Adelaide glowers at me. "If you kick me I swear I'll kill you."

I laugh softly and close my eyes.

I open my eyes a split second before Ara opens my door.

"My head almost hit the ground!" I complain as she laughs crazily.

"The key word is almost," she replies. "You could've, but the important thing is that you didn't."

While walking toward the entrance, I talk to Adelaide. "I retract my previous statement. You don't have to be philosophically competent to enroll in Rookwood. You have to be *completely insane*."

Admission to the aquarium doesn't take long. "I'm surprised that more people aren't here," Zaidan says. He is quivering with excitement, and I decide to talk to him a little bit to ease his nerves.

"Hey," I say. "I think some of the fish we see in there, you might be cooking in a few short years."

He laughs an octave higher than he usually does, an indicator of nervousness. "Troye," he looks at me with a worried look in his eyes. "Do you think it'll work? The whole thing with Ara staying here while I'm in Chicago?"

I make direct eye contact. "I'm positive."

He smiles at me gratefully and then catches up to Ara and Adelaide. In a moment, so do I. They have reached the first tank.

"Beautiful creatures, aren't they?" Adelaide murmurs. "Jellyfish."

I stand next to her in front of the tank. The rest of the room is dark, and the water is colored blue by the indescribable iridescence of the jellyfish.

"Majestic," I say.

"They fascinate me," she states. "Just everything about them; absolutely intriguing."

I look at her, and I can see the reflection of the blueish, glowing creatures in her eyes. She has tilted her head slightly, and she looks mystified. She looks completely different, her skin a cobalt blue. The reflection is gone when Ara tugs on her shoulder.

"Come on," she says to both of us. "We have a time limit. It's going to take eight hours with stops to get to Tampa."

That brings another important question to my mind as we are in a transparent tunnel with moving fish everywhere we look.

"Guys," I say loudly, getting their attention. "If we leave for Tampa tonight, who's driving?"

"I can do it," Zaidan says.

"But you'd have to stay awake all night," Adelaide says worriedly.

"It's fine," Zaidan assures.

I know that it isn't. He is visibly tired, his posture sagging a bit more than usual.

"I'll do it," I offer suddenly. The three of them look alarmed. "It'll give me driving experience," I add hopefully.

"Yeah, but we're going to have to have someone to chaperone him. All night."

"Not it," Zaidan and Ara blurt out simultaneously. The three of us look at Adelaide.

"Oh, all right," she says, resigned.

"It won't be that bad." I defend my driving skills.

She doesn't answer; she is staring at several species of fish. Her eyes look abnormally large, as if they are processing everything all at once.

"Come on," Zaidan urges us. "We don't have a lot of time."

"Okay, okay," Adelaide says, tearing her eyes from her surroundings.

"Troye, are you cold?" Adelaide asks after a couple of minutes of walking aimlessly.

"Not really," I say. I am wearing a white T-shirt and a flannel plaid shirt, as usual. I don't care how hot it is.

Adelaide is wearing a gray T-shirt. "This is a really weird request, but do you mind if I wear your plaid shirt? I'm freezing."

"Oh." It takes me a moment to process her question. "Um, sure."

The shirt is too big for her, so she rolls the sleeves up. When Ara looks back, she raises her eyebrows and I shrug. She faces forward once more with a small smile on her face. I can see Adelaide roll her eyes beside me.

The next few exhibits pass in comfortable silence. I recall bits and pieces from my trip here last year. I was finally away from home . . .

Maybe that's the reason I have such an affinity for Georgia. It's a place where I finally found independence from my family, especially my father.

"Okay?" Adelaide asks.

I nod in affirmation.

"Right." She doesn't sound convinced. This reminds me of the night when we first went to the Tower, when Adelaide wished that I was fine.

"You don't believe me." It is not a question.

"No." It is an answer to a question that never existed.

"Why?" I ask.

She scoffs. "If there is one thing I'm bad at, Troye, it's reading people's faces. I can't do that. But you, however . . ." She looks at me with a peculiar look. "You're as easy to read as a book."

I'm not sure what to say, so I add a humorous spin to the intense dialogue.

"Well, some books are hard to read, Adelaide. May I remind you of *War and Peace*?" I smirk.

"It takes two reads to understand *War and Peace*." Adelaide is not at all hesitant to respond wittily. "It barely takes me half a glance to read you."

"Really?" I face her and cross my arms. "This is definitely more than half a glance. Tell me what you see."

She stares at me calculatingly, crossing her arms as well. After a moment, she opens her mouth. "I think I know. But I'm afraid I'm right."

With a meaningful look she turns on her heel and goes to talk to Ara.

Zaidan taps me on the shoulder. "You okay?"

I nod. "Yeah," I say nonchalantly, shoving my hands into my front pockets. "Let's go."

We're sitting in a dining area, surrounded by noisy people and the semi-pleasant aroma of food, when Zaidan has an epiphany.

"I can't believe it," he states. He looks almost furious.

"What?" Ara teases. "Food not good enough for you, Chef?"

"No." He rolls his eyes at her. "I—We—We're growing up."

"Congratulations," Adelaide says sarcastically. "You've finally got it!"

I tap her arm lightly. "Tact," I say.

She looks sheepish. "Right. Sorry."

"It's fine," Zaidan answers for me. "But I can't get over the fact that I'm moving to Chicago. I'm going to culinary school. Adelaide is becoming an engineer. Troye and Ara, you two . . ." He chuckles. "You two are becoming *doctors*." He emphasizes the word severely.

Ara shakes her head and giggles. "I think you might need a doctor right now."

We are all quiet while we eat, the white noise that has been drifting in our ears taking center stage with no more conversation to barge in and steal the show. That is, until Zaidan starts talking. Zaidan's mind goes a million miles per hour. In this case, his mouth is doing the same thing.

"—and if we look at a couple more exhibits and stall a little bit, then we should head out at eight."

The rest of us nod in affirmation of the meticulous plan that Zaidan has orchestrated.

Zaidan stands up triumphantly. "Let's head out, Quirky Quartet! We've got places to go, things to do!" he says in a deep superhero voice. A little boy sitting in a high chair at the table next to us spills chocolate milk all over his clothes, doubling up with laughter.

Zaidan lowers his voice so only we can hear him. "Okay, now we've really got to go, before his mom kills us for making him spill his milk."

We clean up the table as best as we can, as there are so many people waiting for a table that the poor custodians can't possibly clean every single table in time. I see a mother give us a grateful glance while setting her child down in a previously occupied seat. I give her a small smile.

What takes the smile off my face is seeing the woman rubbing furiously at her son's stained shirt, glaring at Zaidan profusely.

I'm immersed in my thoughts, not paying attention to any of the other exhibits. This makes me feel ridiculously guilty, though I can't fathom why. I explain my predicament to Adelaide.

"Well," she says thoughtfully, "You could be feeling guilty because the species of fish, or whatever the animal may be, are trapped inside the tank for the sensibly determined sole reason of being looked at by visitors. You, as a visitor, are inclined to look at them with interest as that is the most noticeable purpose for their existence here."

"Okay, I think I'm done. How about you?" Ara says, saving me from having to rationalize Adelaide's absurd theory.

"I think I am too," I say. "Shall we go do something unproductive until eight?"

"Sounds brilliant," Zaidan says.

The air is more comfortable as night creeps in. We are sitting right over a patch of almost artificially green grass on a thin blanket we have spread out. It is not quite sunset yet, but the minutes tick slowly by until its arrival. The sky is separated unevenly into various hues of blue, vibrant reds, yellows, oranges, and dark shades of gray where the sun has ceased to reach. Minutes pass. It seems the sky is stuck like this, deciding which form it will take. I wait for the decision of night to be made.

"It's not going to happen while we're still here," Adelaide tells me. "The sunset. It's a summer night; I don't think the sun's going to set for another hour or two."

"You should've told me that earlier," I say. "I would've stopped waiting."

"Your loss of time," Adelaide replies.

"Not really." I shrug my shoulders. "I mean, what else would I be doing?"

"You have a point."

"I usually do."

She could respond with a witty remark but she doesn't. We still have half an hour to wait out before we leave. I lie down. I am too tall for my head to land on the blanket. I can feel the individual blades of grass prickle my neck and ears. The smell of raw earth is stronger now, filling my nose with sharp smells. It is at times like these that I feel most okay with my life. The heaviness from carrying the weight of my own little world on my shoulders seems to dissipate for just a few minutes, and it is the best feeling in the world to just *be there*. I close my eyes, which are suddenly dragged down with a dry, tiresome fatigue that wasn't here a minute ago.

In what seems like a single heartbeat, Adelaide, like many times before, is shaking me awake.

"Good thing you got some rest," she says, tiptoeing and brushing blades of grass from my hair. "We have a long drive to take."

Much to the confusion of the rest of us, who are walking at a leisurely pace, Zaidan rushes toward the car. At first I assume it is because he wants to be on schedule, but then he opens the backseat door for Ara and simpers sloppily, giving her a clumsy bow.

"M'lady," he says in an affected voice.

I think about what kind of person Zaidan is. People who are born strong for others are some of the best, but people who are born weak and grow to be strong for the sake of others are immeasurably rare. I am glad to say that I have found one of those special people in Zaidan.

Right before shutting his door, he tosses his car key to me. Well, I was the intended target. It would've seemed cool and nonchalant had I responded to his action by actually catching the keys. Instead, they are too far left, although I still try to get them and end up scraping my knee. When I look up, I see the key pressed into Adelaide's palm. She smirks.

I stand up. "Not a word," I mutter.

"Then a couple of laughs will do instead, right?" She points at the car, where Ara and Zaidan are laughing hysterically.

"I hate all of you," I mutter, opening the car door jerkily.

"We know," Adelaide tells me. "It's endearing."

We are on the road for only about ten minutes when Zaidan is asleep.

"What can I say? He's a deep sleeper; it comes from being so jumpy all the time," Ara states, pulling Zaidan's head into her lap. He shifts a bit because of the sudden movement, but eventually settles down, his breathing slow and even. Ara shuts her eyes a couple of minutes after the conversation dies. It remains silent for what seems like hours, the only soundtrack the soft breathing of the passengers of the car.

"Mind if I put some music on?" Adelaide asks. "It's quiet, so I think it'll keep them asleep."

"Sure," I say. My eyes are glued to the road. This is the first time I have driven this far, and it'll do me good not to screw anything up during this time period.

"Zaidan's AUX doesn't work," Adelaide whispers. "I guess I'll just play it off my phone."

I hear delicate notes, despite the quiet quality of the sound emitting from the device.

"'Moonlight Sonata' . . ." I murmur. "Beethoven . . . First movement?"

Adelaide nods. "Spot on. Good job, Troye."

"Thanks," I say. "Although I have to admit, I might fall asleep because of it. This is still a really nice piece, though."

Adelaide nods. "Understandable." She is wringing her hands. "I have a hard time sleeping, so I use it to sleep."

"You have a hard time sleeping?" I ask.

She puts a hand on the back of her neck. "Yeah . . . It started a couple of months into freshman year."

"Stress?"

Adelaide nods. "I was overwhelmed by the amount of work it takes to make it into college."

"At least you made it to college. You're going to Georgia Tech in the fall."

"Yeah, I guess." She doesn't sound very sure of herself, a side of Adelaide which is still rare and strange for me to see.

I try to encourage her. "Listen, Adelaide. The first time I met you, I thought you were incredible. I know you hate getting compliments, but this is something you need to hear. You have such a solid exterior, but I know there are things that you hate about yourself. That's what makes you human. Relish in those things and enjoy your humanity. It'll do you good."

Adelaide gulps. "Thanks, Troye," she says in a fragile voice.

"You don't have to be strong all the time," I tell her. "It's not possible."

She smiles sadly. Her eyes are watery and bright, full of thoughts whizzing around and refusing to remain static. "I know," she says. "I really do."

I do not respond. I think this is one of the moments when she needs time to have a conversation with herself without interruption.

"When I was fourteen," she starts, shattering the silence. "I yelled at my mom for the first time. She had scolded me many times before, of course, but this was the first time I said anything back." She fidgets in her seat, and I can tell she is slightly uncomfortable with telling me this. "I wanted to know how it felt, to be the one that yells for once, and not the one who listens."

"And?" I ask. I'm intrigued. I don't know much about Adelaide's life before she met me.

"I vowed to myself afterward that I would never yell at my mother again." She shrugs.

"And I think I've told you this story before to explain why I don't curse. The Tower, remember?"

I nod.

"It escalated after that. I didn't want to let anyone I cared about be vulnerable to things that might harm them. I thought I needed to take the hit for people I love," she adds.

"That's noble."

"And foolish," she adds.

"However foolish it may be, you must admit that it is noble," I reiterate.

"I never said it isn't."

"You never said it is."

After a short pause, she replies, "This conversation is pointless."

I laugh. "Indeed it is." Then I ask a question. "Why are you telling me this?"

"Because I trust you," she replies.

There is another pause.

"Troye, do you mind if I sleep? I'm exhausted."

"No." I take a sip of water. "I'm not tired anyway."

She sounds relieved. "Thanks. Wake me up if you need anything."

"I will," I assure her.

We have five hours left in our journey. I can stay awake without anyone to talk to for that long.

I didn't get a chance to see the sunset in front of the Georgia Aquarium, but we arrive too early for the sunrise in Tampa. We are checking into a hotel, Zaidan tells me. He woke up an hour ago because apparently I "drive too jerkily" to let him get a decent night's sleep.

It's when I pull into a parking lot in front of a posh hotel that I ask Zaidan how the hell we're paying for any of this. He holds up his wallet. "I'm paying for gas and the room, and you guys split the bill between everything else."

I'm about to protest and try to chip in when he stops me. "Shut up, Washingturd. Rule number one in life: when someone's offering you something you need for free, always take it and don't complain."

I shrug. "Okay, I concede."

I shake Adelaide's shoulders gently. "Adelaide," I whisper. "We're here."

She opens her eyes blearily. "We're here?" she repeats, still disoriented.

"Yes," I say. "We're checking in now."

She sits up and rubs her eyes. "Let's go," she yawns.

We all collect our belongings, although Zaidan leaves most of his baggage in the car, all ready for Chicago. "No point in taking it inside and then bringing it back out," he told us sleepily.

I must admit, it is nice to be back home.

We must look odd to the hotel staff. It is really early in the morning, and even though we all look scruffy and haphazard, Zaidan strolls up to the front desk confidently. He greets the man sitting there with extreme politeness and formality. This seems to appease the man, and he seems significantly more pleased with our arrival. He hands Zaidan four key cards.

"I hope you won't be playing those in the hotel room." He eyes Adelaide's violin case and my viola case warily.

"Oh, of course not, sir." Adelaide is the epitome of respect. I give him a nod.

He is satisfied with our promises. "Have a nice night!" he calls after us.

"Thank you," Ara responds enthusiastically.

In the elevator, Adelaide laughs out of the blue.

"What is it?" I ask.

"The elevator music," she says. "It's one of Mozart's piano sonatas."

I chuckle, partially because I find it amusing, and partially because I am reaching the point where I am so tired that everything is becoming humorous.

We only have one room. ("I might be paying, but we're still on a tight budget," Zaidan defends himself.) Zaidan and Ara claim one bed, and slide in immediately, not bothering to change their clothes. Adelaide, however, insists on taking a shower first. "I look like death," she complains.

"You really don't," I say while handing her a fluffy white towel.

"Nice try," she responds right before slamming the door.

I impulsively get out my phone. No notifications. I am satisfied that my mother isn't having a meltdown about me not responding to any of her texts.

Just got to Tampa right now. How are you? I text her, just in case.

I am asleep before Adelaide finishes her shower.

"Rise and shine, Washingturd!" Zaidan's voice is annoyingly happy.

I groan. "Get out, Zaidan."

I feel a pillow slam into the side of my head forcefully. "Get up, Troye!" He practically sings. "We are in the land where you were born, and we expect a tour."

"Give me an hour," I try to negotiate.

"No, I don't think—Troye, you got a text."

I am up in no time. I grab my phone from Zaidan. It's my mom; she responded at an ungodly time during the night.

Good to hear that you're not dead, Troye, though I would've been fooled until your last text.

Haha, very funny. I'll talk to you later. We're headed to Conundrum, I think.

Good restaurant, she writes. *Have fun!*

"So, what are we doing today?" Ara asks, stretching her arms upward.

"I know this really nice place that serves good breakfast," I say. "It's called Conundrum."

"Sounds cool." Adelaide, fresh out of the bathroom, sits next to me on the bed. "Shall we go now?"

"Okay," I say, standing up. "Conundrum it is."

The rest of the day passes normally. I show them my old house and we take long walks around my old neighborhood. My house, although in good condition, has still not been sold and remains barren and vacant.

It is a warm, humid night, and we have just arrived back at the hotel. The elevator doors are about to close when a bellhop sticks his foot out to prevent them from doing so.

"Is one of you a Mr. Troye Saavedra?" he asks.

I give him a little wave. "That'd be me."

He hands me an envelope. "This is for you."

"Um . . . Thank you," I tell him.

"No problem, sir." He gives us a grin and then heads back to the lobby, allowing the doors to close of their own accord.

"I wonder what it is," Adelaide says, sounding curious even though we are all extremely fatigued.

"I don't know," I say sleepily. "I'll just open it in the morning."

No one seems discontent with that idea.

"Screw the shower," Adelaide mumbles when we trudge through the halls of our floor, headed toward our delightful beds. "I need sleep."

"I completely agree with that idea," I mutter.

Zaidan opens the heavy door gratefully, and we all sink into bed. The letter lies on the bedside table, to be forgotten until the morning.

I'm the first to wake in the morning, even before Adelaide. I check the alarm clock, careful not to wake any of the others. It's about five, and Adelaide will be up in two hours minimum. In my peripheral vision I see the letter that was handed to me last night, still unopened. I shrug. Why not?

The crinkling of the paper is insurmountably loud, intermingled with the deafening silence of the room. I read the letter silently. Then, without any wasted effort, I fold it up gently and put it in my pocket. I grab the pad of paper and pen that the hotel has provided from the desk.

I've gone out for a bit. Don't look for me, and don't wait for me. -Troye

Satisfied with my cryptic note, I grab my viola case and my phone from its charger. Slipping the phone in my pocket and slinging the case over my back, I try to shut the door quietly. The noise reverberating off the floor seems gargantuan and clunky because there is no other noise to cover their tracks.

My mother calls. She usually never calls anyone; she prefers texting to anything else on her phone.

"Troye?" Her voice sounds panicked, and she hiccups around every other sentence.

"Mom."

"It's Ivan. He's not been near the house, and I haven't seen him since you left. This is really irrational of me, but just keep an eye out."

My breath hitches, and it feels like hot coals have forced their way into my throat.

"It's okay. I think I already know where he is." My throat feels uncomfortably constricted.

I walk rather than taking Zaidan's car. It feels more natural. There is a warm fog hovering over the area, but it is sure to dissipate by sunrise. There aren't many people on the streets, and all is quiet. I walk aimlessly until I know exactly where I'm going. I am headed to my home, with its large halls and my brown room and my secret place. I know the ladder is long gone, but I find, surprisingly, that the front door is unlocked.

A cascade of memories hits me as I enter the house again. It has been completely repainted, all the walls once more a horrendous white. But nevertheless, it is still recognizable.

I walk up the stairs, abandoning my tradition of always running up stairs. This time, I decide, I need to take my time. Even though I have not been here in a year, I still automatically skip the creaky stair. Your body, I note, can remember things long after you yourself have forgotten them.

My room's carpet is still the same, and I can almost smell the whiskey my father spilled what seems like decades ago. The walls, however, like the rest of the house, are white. I cannot stand it. It is unacceptable. I set my viola case on the floor and open it up, tuning the instrument and tightening the bow hair.

Dear Troye,

I know you hate me right now, and you've gotten sick of reading notes like this.

The first few notes I play of a song that has never existed are raspy. They are slow and melodious, sinking in after ages of playing them over and over again.

But the thing is, I am a very selfish person. You're not. It's a relationship that was supposed to work perfectly, but then it just . . . didn't.

The notes come with more urgency now, faster and louder.

I think it was alcohol that stole what we had, and forced us apart. Yes, it was definitely her. Oh, who am I kidding? It's me. It's my fault.

I press the bow onto the strings with more vigor, trying to make the sound loud enough to drown my thoughts.

I'm sorry for that. I hate to say it so bluntly, but I have to say it.

I can see some of the bow's hairs coming loose from the force.

You left me, at least emotionally. You were gone. So was your mother. I know it's not your fault, and I'm not saying it is. I'm just scared. You looked so happy these past few weeks, so unconcerned with the fact that I wasn't a part of your life anymore. What was I supposed to do?

The hairs are starting come completely off.

After you were gone, I wasn't able to maintain any other relationships I had. Even Lavinia left. I couldn't stand it. I still can't.

I am going to break my bow at this rate.

I've never really written my feelings in a concrete sort of way, but I guess this is the first and last time I'm going to get to say what I feel. After all, a person who has already given up on himself should have no problem writing a suicide note.

The bow hits the ground, almost snapping in half. I don't care.

Remember me well,

Dad

My viola slips from my hands, splintering on impact of the floor.

Silence Interrupted

I sit on the floor between the bent strings and the snapped bridge and the shards of thick wood, in the graveyard of my viola. I have played with this instrument for the past eight years. I will never use it again. It is damaged beyond repair. I deserve this, I think. I deserve the pain. But do I really?

I hate drunkards. I always have. My father was one, and I lost all respect for him. But how can I hate him? How can I hate the person who taught me how to play chess in third grade, who tutored me in AP classes that I'd have failed without him? How can I hate a person who used to be my best friend? I know why I can hate him, and for this, I deserve the pain. I hate myself—a bigoted, egotistical maniac, who thought that everything could be so black and white. In the end, nothing and no one is ever that simple, including people like my father.

I sweep up the various parts of the viola with my hand and dump them into the case, wincing as the parts rattle when I pick the case up.

I find his body on the floor of what used to be their master bedroom, one hand folded smartly on the abdomen and the other dangling off to the side. There are two empty bottles, pills whose names I can't pronounce. I know that's not what actually killed him.

I insist to Adelaide, Ara, and Zaidan to stay at the hotel, and only Adelaide convinces me to let her come with me.

He has stopped suffering, they say. My mom is crying while his old bar friends look on in disbelief. It's a sunny day. Days are not usually sunny when people die. Then again, people die all the time. There have to be some beautiful days with dead bodies.

Goddammit.

Why does he look so small in that coffin? He's a lanky guy, taller than I am, in fact. Will I look that small in a coffin? I sure hope not. I laugh internally. *Troye, you're at your dad's funeral and all you're thinking about is if you're going to look small at your own funeral. Don't be so vain.*

I think I'm going insane.

This graveyard is old. He shouldn't be here. But Goddammit. He is here, and it is horrible.

Everyone is dressed in black, and they all look the same: a mass of ostensibly uncaring people who look exactly alike. Why the hell are they here? They don't care anyway. I see a man with a Bluetooth earpiece, talking quietly but intensely to his "unqualified" employee, from what I overhear.

A child tugs on the hem of her mother's shirt. "Can we go now?" she says.

Her mother shushes her child. "Don't ask again!" she hisses.

Adelaide drags me away, gripping my hand so hard that I fear my bones will actually break. Ivan looks so pale, so weak and helpless. I can still hear his voice. I can still hear his laughter. His eyes are shut.

I will never see them again.

I see them from afar, lowering his coffin into the previously dug six-foot hole. Adelaide grips my hand tightly again. I wipe my eyes.

I didn't really care what happened to him after the divorce. I think that I subconsciously thought he would be fine, that the drinking only affected my mom and me. I didn't know he was so attached, so easily disturbed. This is what humans do, and it is one of our main flaws: we can't see past problems that affect us.

I'm only human. I can't always be compassionate and caring. Most actions I take are based on my own gain, whether I realize it or not. Sometimes I am too blind to see how I am affecting others around me. Sometimes I am too wrapped up in my own little world to care about the needs of others.

It's just so unfair. I shouldn't feel guilty. I shouldn't. I can still hear the echoes of his taunts, of the maniacal jeering.

I am aware of my actions, but I am painfully unaware of their collateral damage.

It's silent. Quiet is a colorless concept, with no set form. It can choose to be friend or foe, companion or adversary. Silence is always with you, even at the loudest points in your life.

I look at Adelaide before turning back to my father's grave.

About the Author

SANIA SHAIKH IS A JUNIOR AT CAMBRIDGE HIGH SCHOOL. Inspired to write from a young age, she worked on *Silence Interrupted*, her debut novel, starting in eighth grade.